"If this child is mine then I won't dodge my responsibility."

She looked less than impressed by the idea. "If you're talking about money, I think I've made it pretty clear I'm not interested."

"You can't raise a child on good intentions, Mary-Jayne. Be sensible."

She looked ready for an argument, but she seemed to change her mind. "I'm heating up lasagna. Are you staying for dinner?"

Daniel raised a brow. "Am I invited?"

She shrugged, like she couldn't care either way.

"Sure," she said. "That would be good."

He watched as she removed several items from the refrigerator and began making a salad. And Daniel couldn't take his eyes off her. Her glorious hair shone like ebony beneath the kitchen light and she chewed her bottom lip as she completed the task. And of course thinking about her lips made him remember their night together. And kissing her. And making love to her. She had a remarkable effect on him, and he wondered if it was because they were so different that he was so achingly attracted to her. She was all challenge. All resistance. And since very little challenged him these days, Daniel knew her very determination to avoid him had a magnetic pull all of its own.

And he had no idea what he was going to do about it.

THE PRESTONS OF CRYSTAL POINT:
All's fair in family...and love!

Dear Reader,

Hello, and welcome back to Crystal Point and my seventh book for Harlequin Special Edition, *The CEO's Baby Surprise*.

Since the publication of my first Special Edition book, I've had countless emails from readers asking me when the spirited and feisty Mary-Jayne Preston was going to get her own story. I'm delighted that I've been able to give Mary-Jayne her very own happy ending at last! It's not an easy road—not when she falls for a man who is her complete opposite in every way...except, of course, in the way which counts the most. The hero, Daniel, gets a whole lot more than he bargains for when he meets the free-spirited Mary-Jayne. Including a couple of very big surprises along the way!

I hope you enjoy *The CEO's Baby Surprise* and wish you a few hours of happy reading. For more of my Crystal Point books please visit my author page at harlequin.com.

I love hearing from readers and can be contacted via my website at helenlacey.com.

Warm wishes,

Helen Lacey

The CEO's
Baby Surprise

——

Helen Lacey

HARLEQUIN® SPECIAL EDITION®

Recycling programs
for this product may
not exist in your area.

ISBN-13: 978-0-373-65880-0

The CEO's Baby Surprise

Copyright © 2015 by Helen Lacey

Printed in U.S.A.

Helen Lacey grew up reading *Black Beauty* and *Little House on the Prairie*. These childhood classics inspired her to write her first book when she was seven, a story about a girl and her horse. She loves writing for Harlequin Special Edition, where she can create strong heroes with a soft heart and heroines with gumption who get their happily-ever-after. For more about Helen, visit her website, helenlacey.com.

Books by Helen Lacey

Harlequin Special Edition

The Prestons of Crystal Point

The CEO's Baby Surprise
Claiming His Brother's Baby
Once Upon a Bride
Date with Destiny
His-and-Hers Family
Marriage Under the Mistletoe
Made for Marriage

Visit the Author Profile page at Harlequin.com for more titles.

For my mother, Evelyn.
Who believes in me no matter what.

Prologue

Mary-Jayne Preston yawned, opened her eyes and blinked a few times. The ceiling spun fractionally, and she drew in a soft breath.

I'm not hungover.

She closed her eyes again. The two glasses of champagne she'd drunk the night before weren't responsible for the way she felt. This was something else. An unusual lethargy crept into her limbs and spread across her skin. Her lids fluttered, and she glimpsed a sliver of light from between heavy drapes.

An unfamiliar room.

Her memory kicked in. The Sandwhisper Resort. Port Douglas.

But this isn't my bedroom.

This was a villa suite. And a top-end one, judging by the plush feel of the giant king-size bed and lavish damask drapes. Extravagance personified. Her eyelids drooped before opening again as she stretched her spine—and then nearly jumped out of her skin when she realized she wasn't alone in the big bed.

A man lay beside her. She twisted her head and saw a long, perfectly proportioned back. Smooth skin, like the sheerest satin stretched over pressed steel, broad shoulders, strong arms and dark hair. He lay on his stomach, one arm flung above his head, the other curved by his side. And he was asleep. The soft rhythm of his breathing was oddly hypnotic, and she stared at him, suddenly mesmerized by his bronzed skin and lean, muscular frame.

And then, in stunning Technicolor, it came rushing back.

The party.

The kiss.

The one-night stand.

Her first. Her *last*.

She needed to get up. To *think*. She shimmied sideways but quickly stopped moving when he stirred. She wasn't quite ready for any kind of face-to-face, morning-after awkwardness. Not with *him*. She took a deep breath and tried again, inching her hips across the cool sheet so slowly it was agonizing. Finally one leg found the edge of the mattress and she pushed the cover back. He moved again and she stilled instantly. He made a sound, half groan, half moan, and flipped around, the sheet draping haphazardly over his hips as he came to face her.

But still asleep.

Mary-Jayne's breath shuddered out as she caught sight of his profile. He was ridiculously handsome. No wonder she'd lost her head. The straight nose, chiseled cheeks and square jaw was a riveting combination. And she quickly recalled those silver-gray eyes of his…just too sexy for words. As her gaze traveled lower her fingertips tingled.

His body was incredibly well cut, and she fought the urge to touch him just one more time. She spotted a faint mark on his shoulder. Like a love bite.

Did I do that?

Heat surged through her blood when she remembered what they'd done the night before, and again in the small hours of the morning. No sweet wonder her muscles ached and her skin seemed ultrasensitive. She'd never had a night like it before, never felt such intense desire or experienced such acute and mindboggling pleasure.

It was like a dream. A fantasy.

And she needed to wake up from this particular dream. Quickly.

She managed to ease off the bed and quickly looked around for her clothes. Her underwear was by the bed, and she snatched it up with guilty fingers and then quickly dressed into the thong and bra. The shoes were easily spotted—one was by the window, the other under a chair in the corner of the room. But the black dress was nowhere to be seen. The smooth fabric had clung to her curves, and the man in the bed had told her how beautiful and desirable she'd looked. No one had ever said those words quite that way to her before. She found her purse on the chair and continued looking for the dress, keeping a mindful eye on him.

Please don't wake up...

He didn't, thankfully, and a few moments later she found the dress, scrunched in a ball and hidden beneath the quilt that had fallen to the foot of the bed. She stepped into it and slipped it up and over her hips, settling her arms through the bodice before she twisted herself into a pretzel to do up the zipper. Breathless, she cast another look toward the sleeping man.

I'm such a fool...

For weeks she'd stayed resolute, determined to avoid crashing into bed with him. But the moment he'd touched her, the moment he'd made his move she'd melted like an ice cube in hell.

Mary-Jayne pushed her feet into her patent pumps, grabbed her purse and ran.

Chapter One

*P*regnant.

Not a bout of food poisoning as she'd wanted to believe.

Mary-Jayne walked from the doctor's office and headed for her car. Her head hurt. Her feet hurt. Everything hurt. The snap on her jeans felt tight around her waist. Now she knew why.

She was three months and three weeks pregnant.

She opened the door of the borrowed Honda Civic and got inside. Then she placed a hand over her belly and let out a long, heavy breath.

Twenty-seven. Single. Pregnant.

Right.

Not exactly the end of the world…but not what she'd been expecting, either.

One day she'd imagined she'd have a baby. When she was married and settled, not while she was trying to carve out a career as a jewelry designer and wasn't exactly financially stable.

She thought about calling her older sisters, Evie and Grace, but quickly shrugged off the idea. She needed time to think. Plan. Sort out what she was going to do, before she told anyone. Especially her sisters, who'd want to know *everything*.

She'd have to tell them about that night.

She gripped the steering wheel and let out a long, weary sigh. She'd tried to put the memory from her mind countless times. And failed. Every time she walked around the grounds of the Sandwhisper Resort she was reminded. And every time she fielded a telephone call from *him* she was thrust back to that crazy night.

Mary-Jayne drove through the gates of the resort and took a left down the road that led to the employees' residences. Her villa was small but well appointed and opened onto the deck and to the huge heated pool and spa area. The Sandwhisper Resort was one of the largest in Port Douglas, and certainly one of the most luxurious. The town of Port Douglas was about forty miles north of Cairns, and its population of over three thousand often doubled during peak vacation times. Living and working at the luxurious resort for the past four and half months hadn't exactly been a hardship. Running her friend Audrey's boutique was mostly enjoyable and gave her the opportunity to create and showcase her own jewelry. Life was a breeze.

Correction.

Life *had* been a breeze.

Until she'd had an uncharacteristic one-night stand with Daniel Anderson.

CEO of Anderson Holdings and heir apparent to the huge fortune that had been made by his grandfather from ore and copper mining years earlier, he owned the Sandwhisper Resort with his two brothers. There were four other resorts around the globe—one in Phuket, another along the Amalfi coast in Italy, another in the Maldives and the flagship resort in the San Francisco Bay Area.

He was rich, successful, uptight and absurdly arrogant. Everything she'd always abhorred in a man.

He was also reported to be kind, generous and honest.

Well…according to his grandmother.

Eighty-year-old Solana Anderson adored her grandsons and spent her retirement flying between the east and west coasts of Australia and America, living at the resorts during the spring and summer months in alternating time zones. Mary-Jayne liked the older woman very much. They'd met the first day she'd arrived at the resort after the desperate emergency call from her old school friend Audrey had sent her flying up to Port Douglas with barely a packed suitcase. Audrey had moved into Mary-Jayne's small house in Crystal Point so she could be close to her ill mother while Mary-Jayne moved into Audrey's condo at the resort. Once she was in residence, she read the scribbled note with instructions her friend had left and opened the boutique at an unrespectable eleven o'clock. It was meant to be a temporary gig—but Audrey insisted her mother needed her. So her planned three weeks ended up being for six months.

And Solana, straight backed and still vibrant at nearly eighty years of age, had come into the store looking for an outfit to wear to her upcoming birthday party, and within the hour they were chatting and laughing over herbal tea and several outfit changes. It was then she learned that Solana's American-born husband had died a decade earlier and how she'd borne him a son and daughter. Mary-Jayne had listened while Solana talked about her much-loved grandsons, Daniel, Blake and Caleb and granddaughter Renee. One hour ticked over into two, and by three o'clock the older woman had finally decided upon an outfit and persuaded Mary-Jayne to let her see some of her hand-crafted jewelry pieces. Solana had since bought three items and had recommended Mary-Jayne's work to several of her friends.

Yes, she liked Solana. But wasn't about to tell the other woman she was carrying her great-grandchild. Not until she figured out what she was going to do. She was nearly four months along, and her pregnancy would be showing itself very soon. She couldn't hide her growing stomach behind baggy clothes forever.

He has a right to know...

The notion niggled at her over and over.

She could have the baby alone. Women did it all the time. And it was not as if she and Daniel had any kind of relationship. If she wanted, she could leave the resort and go home and never see him again. He lived mostly in San Francisco. She lived in Crystal Point, a small seaside town that sat at the southernmost point of the Great Barrier Reef. They had different lives. Different worlds.

And she didn't even like him.

She'd met him three times before the night of Solana's birthday. The first time she'd been in the store window, bent over and struggling to remove a garment from the mannequin. When she was done she'd straightened, turned to avoid knocking the mannequin over and came face-to-face with him on the other side of the glass. He'd been watching her, arms crossed.

Of course she'd known immediately who he was. There were several pictures of him and his brothers in Solana's villa, and she'd visited the older woman many times. Plus, he looked enough like his younger brother Caleb for her to recognize the family resemblance. Caleb ran the resorts in Port Douglas and Phuket while his twin Blake looked after Amalfi, Maldives and San Francisco. And according to staff gossip Daniel lorded over the resorts, his brothers and the staff from his private jet.

Still, it was hard not to be impressed by his ridiculous good looks, and despite the fact he was not her type, Mary-Jayne was as susceptible as the next woman. The impeccably cut suit, creaseless white shirt and dark tie were a riveting combination on his broad, tall frame, and for a second she'd been rooted to the spot, unable to move, unable to do anything other than stare back, held captive by the look in his gray eyes. For a moment, at least. Until he'd raised one brow and a tiny smile whispered along the edges of his mouth. He'd then looked her over with a kind of leisurely conceit that had quickly sent alarm bells clanging in her head.

There'd been interest in his expression and if he'd been anyone else she might have made some kind of encouraging gesture. Like a smile. Or nod. But Daniel Anderson was out of her league. A rich and successful corporate shark with a reputation for having no tolerance for fools in business, and no proclivity for commitment in his private life. He was the kind of man she'd always planned to avoid like the plague. The kind of man that had never interested her before.

But something had passed between them in that first moment. A look… Recognition.

Awareness…

Heat…

Attraction…

When her good sense had returned she'd darted from the window and got back to the customer waiting in the changing room. By the time she'd moved back to the front of the store and began ringing up the sale he was gone.

Mary-Jayne saw him a day later, striding across the resort foyer with his brother at his side. She'd been coming from the day spa, arms loaded with jewelry trays, when Caleb had said her name. She'd met the younger Anderson many times over the previous weeks. He was rich, charming and handsome and didn't do a solitary thing to her libido. Not so his older brother. She'd fumbled with the trays and stayed rooted to the spot as they approached and then managed to nod her way through an introduction. He was unsmiling, but his eyes regarded her with blistering intensity. Caleb's attention had quickly been diverted by the day-shift concierge and she'd been left alone with him, silent and nervous beneath his unfaltering gaze.

Then he'd spoken, and his deep voice, a smooth mix of his American upbringing and Australian roots, wound up her spine like liquid silk. "My grandmother tells me you're here for six months rather than the few weeks you'd originally planned on?"

He'd talked about her with Solana? "Ah, that's right," she'd croaked.

"And are you enjoying your time here?"

She'd nodded, feeling stupid and awkward and not in the least bit like her usual self. Normally she was confident and opinionated and more than comfortable in her own skin. But two seconds around Daniel Anderson and she was a speechless fool. Übergood looks had never interested her before. But he stirred her senses big time.

"Yes, very much."

"And I trust your friend's parent's health is improving?"

He knew about Audrey's mother? Solana *had* been busy sharing information.

"A little…yes."

A small smile had crinkled the corner of his mouth and Mary-Jayne's gaze had instantly been drawn to his lips. He had seen her reaction and his smile had increased fractionally. There was something extraordinarily hypnotic about him, something she couldn't quite fathom. Something she'd known she had to extricate herself from…and fast.

She'd hastily excused herself and taken off as fast as she could.

And hadn't seen him again for two days.

She'd left the resort for a run along the beach and had come upon him jogging in the other direction. He'd slowed when he was about twenty feet from her and come to a halt right next to her. And the look between them had been electric. Out of this world and all-consuming. She'd never experienced such blatant and blistering physical attraction for anyone before. And it shocked her to the core. He wasn't her usual type. In fact, Daniel Anderson was the epitome of everything she *didn't* want in a man. Money, power, arrogance… They were attributes her small-town, middle-class self had decided long ago were not for her. She dated musicians and out-of-work artists. Not corporate sharks.

His expression had been unwavering and contained hot sexual appreciation. He wanted her. No doubt about it. And the look in his eyes had made it clear he thought he'd get her.

"You know," he'd said with a kind of arrogant confidence that made her tremble. "My villa is only minutes away."

She knew that. The family's quarters were secluded and luxurious and away from the main part of the resort and had a spectacular view of the beach.

"And?" she'd managed to say, despite the way her heart had thundered behind her ribs and her knees wobbled.

He'd half smiled. "And we both know that's where we're going to end up at some point."

Mortified, she'd quickly taken off like a bullet. But her body was thrumming with a kind of intoxicating awareness that stayed with her for hours. For days. Until she'd seen him again two days later at Solana's birthday party. The older woman had insisted she attend the celebration and Mary-Jayne respected Solana too much to refuse the invitation. She'd ditched her usual multicolored skirts and long tops and rummaged through Audrey's wardrobe for a party dress. And she'd found one—a slip of silky black jersey that clung to her like a second skin. The huge ball-room was easy to get lost in…or so she'd thought. But it had only taken ten minutes until she'd felt him watching her from across the room. He'd approached and asked if she wanted a drink. Within half an hour they had been out on the balcony, talking intimately. Seconds later they'd been kissing madly. Minutes later they'd been in his villa tearing each other's clothes off.

But Mary-Jayne wasn't under any illusions.

She knew enough about Daniel Anderson to realize she was simply another notch on his bedpost. He was hand-some, successful and wealthy and played the field merci-lessly. Something he had done without compunction since the death of his wife and unborn child four years earlier. He certainly wouldn't be interested in her for anything other than a one-night stand. She wasn't his type. Oh, he'd knocked on the door of her villa the day after Solana's party and asked her out. But she'd shut him down. She'd piqued his interest for a moment and that was all. Thank-fully, he'd left the resort the following day and returned to San Francisco, exactly as she'd hoped. But she hadn't expected that he'd call the store two weeks later and an-nounce that he wanted to see her again when he returned from California.

See her?

Yeah…right. The only thing he wanted to see was her naked body between the sheets. And she knew that for a man like Daniel Anderson, the chase was all that mattered. She'd refused him, and that was like pouring oil onto a fire.

When he'd called her again two weeks later she'd been in South Dakota for a friend's wedding. Annoyed that he wouldn't take the hint and all out of patience, she'd lost her temper and told him to go to hell. Then she'd returned to the Sandwhisper Resort and waited. Waited for another call. Waited for him to arrive at the resort and confuse and seduce her with his steely-eyed gaze and uncompromising intensity. But he hadn't called. And hadn't returned. As one week slipped into another, Mary-Jayne had slowly relaxed and convinced herself he'd lost interest.

Which was exactly what she wanted.

Only now, the tables had turned. She was having his baby. Which meant one thing—she'd have to see him and tell him she was having his baby. And soon.

Daniel had struggled with the remnants of a headache for two days. The three other suits in the conference room were grating on his nerves. Some days he wanted nothing more than to throw off the shackles of his name, his legacy and everything else and live a simple, quiet life.

Like today.

Because it was his birthday. He was turning thirty-four years old. He had money and power and a successful business at his command. He had apartments in San Francisco, another in London and then there was the family-owned hilltop chateau in France that he hadn't been near for over four years. He also had any number of women willing to warm his bed with minimal notice and who understood he didn't want commitment or anything resembling a serious relationship. He traveled the world but rarely saw anything other than the walls of boardrooms and offices at the resorts he'd helped build into some of the most successful around the globe. Nothing and no one touched him.

Well…except for Mary-Jayne Preston.

She was a thorn in his side. A stone in his shoe. A pain in his neck.

Months after that one crazy night in Port Douglas and he was still thinking about her. She was incredibly beautiful. Her green eyes were luminous; her lips were full and endlessly kissable. But it was her hair that had first captured his attention that day in the store window. She had masses of dark curls that hung down past her shoulders. And of course there were her lovely curves, which she possessed in all the right places.

He'd checked out her history and discovered she came from a middle-class family in Crystal Point, had studied at a local technical college and had an online business selling her handcrafted jewelry. She rented her home, owned a dog, volunteered at a number of animal shelters, had strong opinions about the environment and politics and liked to dress in colorful skirts or jeans with holes in the knees. She had piercings in her ears and navel and a butterfly tattoo on one shoulder.

She wasn't his type. Not by a long shot.

Which didn't make one ounce of difference to the relentless effect she had on him whenever she was within a twenty-foot radius. And the night of his grandmother's birthday party he'd almost tripped over his own feet when he'd caught a glimpse of her across the room. She'd looked incredible in a dress that highlighted every dip and curve of her body. And with her dark hair cascading down her back in a wave he just about had to cleave his tongue from the roof of his mouth. She looked hot. Gorgeous. Desirable.

And he knew then he wanted to get her in his bed.

It took half an hour to get her alone. Then he'd kissed her. And she'd kissed him back.

And before either of them had a chance to come up for air they were in his villa suite, tearing off clothes with little finesse and more eagerness than he'd felt in years. It had been a hot, wild night, compounded by months of abstinence and the fact he'd had Mary-Jayne Preston very much on his mind since the first time he'd seen her.

"Are you listening?"

Daniel shook off his thoughts and glanced to his left. Blake was staring at him, one brow cocked. "Always."

Blake didn't look convinced and quickly turned his attention to the other suits in the room. After a few more minutes, he dismissed the two other men, and once they were alone his brother moved to the bar and grabbed two imported beers from the fridge.

Daniel frowned. "A little early, don't you think?"

Blake flicked the tops off the bottles and shrugged. "It's after three. And you look as if you need it."

He didn't disagree, and stretched back in his leather chair. "Maybe I do."

Blake passed him a beer and grabbed a seat. "Happy birthday," his brother said, and clinked the bottle necks.

"Thanks," he said but didn't take a drink. The last thing he wanted to do was add alcohol to the remainders of a blinding headache.

His brother, who was probably the most intuitive person he'd ever known, looked at him as if he knew exactly what he was thinking. "You know, you should go home."

"I live *here*, remember?"

Blake shook his head. "I meant *home*…not here. Port Douglas."

Except Port Douglas didn't feel any more like home than San Francisco, Phuket or Amalfi.

Nowhere did. Not since Simone had died. The bayside condo they'd bought still sat empty, and he lived in a villa at the San Francisco resort when he wasn't at any of the other four locations. He'd been born in Australia and moved to California when he was two years old. The San Francisco resort was the first, which made it home, even though he'd spent most of his adult life shifting between the two countries.

He scowled. "I can't do that right now."

"Why not?" Blake shot back. "Caleb's got the Phuket renovation under control. Things are sweet here in San Francisco." His brother grinned. "You're not really needed. CEOs are kind of superfluous to the running of a company anyhow. We all knew that when Gramps was at the helm."

"Superfluous?"

Blake's grin widened. "Yeah…like the foam on the top of an espresso to go… You know, there but not really necessary."

"You're an ass."

His brother's grin turned into a chuckle. "All I'm saying is that you haven't taken a real break from this gig for years. Not even when…"

Not even when Simone died.

Four years, four months and three weeks ago. Give or take a day. She'd been driving back from a doctor's appointment and had stopped at the mall for some shopping. The brakes on a car traveling in the opposite direction had failed. Simone had suffered terrible injuries and died an hour later in hospital. So had the baby she carried. He'd lost his wife and unborn daughter because of a broken brake line. "I'm fine," he said, and tasted the lie on his tongue.

"I'm pretty sure you're not," Blake said, more serious. "And something's been bugging you the past few months."

Something. Someone. *Green eyes... Black curling hair... Red lips...*

Daniel drank some beer. "You're imagining things. And stop fretting. You're turning into your mother."

His brother laughed loudly. They both knew that Blake was more like their father, Miles, than any of them. Daniel's mother had died of a massive brain hemorrhage barely hours after his birth, and their father had married Bernadette two years later. Within six months the twins, Blake and Caleb, were born. Bernie was a nice woman and had always treated him like her own, and wasn't as vague and hopeless as their father. Business acumen and ambition had skipped a generation, and now Miles spent his time painting and sculpting and living on their small hobby farm an hour west of Port Douglas.

Daniel finished the beer and placed the bottle on the table. "I don't need a vacation."

"Sure you do," Blake replied. "If you don't want to go to Australia, take a break somewhere else. Maybe Fiji? Or what about using that damned mausoleum that sits on that hill just outside Paris? Take some time off, relax, get laid," his brother said, and grinned again. "Recharge like us regular folk have to do every now and then."

"You're as tied to this business as I am."

"Yeah," his brother agreed. "But I know when to quit. I've got my cabin in the woods, remember?"

Blake's *cabin* was a sprawling Western red cedar house nestled on forty hectares he'd bought in small town Colorado a few years back. Daniel had visited once, hated the cold and being snowbound for days on end and decided that a warm climate was more his thing.

"I don't need a—"

"Then, how about you think about what the rest of us need?" Blake said firmly. "Or what Caleb and I need, which isn't you breathing down our necks looking for things we're doing wrong because you're so damned bored and frustrated that you can't get out your own way. Basically, *I* need a break. So go home and get whatever's bugging you out of your system and spend some time with Solana. You know you've always been her favorite."

Daniel looked at his brother. Had he done that? Had he become an overzealous, critical jerk looking for fault in everything and everyone? And bored? Was that what he was? He did miss Solana. He hadn't seen his grandmother since her birthday weekend. And it was excuse enough to see Mary-Jayne again—and get her out of his system once and for all.

He half smiled. "Okay."

Chapter Two

"Everything all right?"

Mary-Jayne nodded and looked up from the plate of food she'd been pretending to give way too much attention. "Fine."

"Are you still feeling unwell?" Solana asked. "You never did tell me what the doctor said."

"Just a twenty-four-hour bug," she replied vaguely. "And I feel fine now."

Solana didn't look convinced. "You're still pale. Is that ex-boyfriend of yours giving you grief?"

The *ex-boyfriend*. The one she'd made up to avoid any nosy questions about what was becoming her rapidly expanding middle. The ex-boyfriend she'd say was the father of her baby until she summoned the nerve to tell Solana she was carrying her grandson's child. Raised to have a solid moral compass, she was torn between believing the father of her baby had a right to know, and the fear that telling him would change everything. She was carrying Solana's great-grandchild. An Anderson heir. Nothing would be the same.

Of course, she had no illusions. Daniel Anderson was not a man looking for commitment or a family. Solana had told her enough about him, from his closed-off heart to his rumored no-strings relationships. He'd lost the love of his life and unborn child and had no interest in replacing, either.

Not that she was interested in him in *that* way. She didn't like him at all. He was arrogant and opinionated and as cold as a Popsicle. Oh, she'd certainly been swept away that one night. But one night of hot and heavy sex didn't make them *anything*.

Still…they'd made a baby together, and as prepared as she was to raise her child alone, common courtesy made it very clear to her that she had to tell him. And soon. Before Solana or anyone else worked out that she was pregnant.

She had another two weeks at the store before Audrey returned, and once that was done, Mary-Jayne intended returning to Crystal Point to regroup and figure out how to tell Daniel he was about to become a father.

"I'm going to miss you when you leave," Solana said and smiled. "I've grown very fond of our talks."

So had Mary-Jayne. She'd become increasingly attached to the other woman over the past few months, and they lunched together at least twice a week. And Solana had been incredibly supportive of her jewelry designing and had even offered to finance her work and help expand the range into several well-known stores around the country. Of course Mary-Jayne had declined the offer. Solana was a generous woman, but she'd never take advantage of their friendship in such a way…good business or not.

"We'll keep in touch," Mary-Jayne assured her and ignored the nausea scratching at her throat. Her appetite had been out of whack for weeks and the sick feeling still hadn't abated even though she was into her second trimester. Her doctor told her not to worry about it and assured her that her appetite would return, and had put her on a series of vitamins. But most days the idea of food before three in the afternoon was unimaginable.

"Yes, we must," Solana said warmly. "Knowing you has made me not miss Renee quite so much," she said of her granddaughter, who resided in London. "Of course, I get to see Caleb while I'm here and Blake when I'm in San Francisco. And Daniel when he's done looking after things and flying in between resorts. But sometimes I wish for those days when they were kids and not spread all over the world." The older woman put down her cutlery and sighed. "Listen to me, babbling on, when you must miss your own family very much."

"I do," she admitted. "I'm really close to my sisters and brother and I miss my parents a lot."

"Naturally." Solana's eyed sparkled. "Family is everything."

Mary-Jayne swallowed the lump of emotion in her throat, like she'd done countless times over the past few months. Her hormones were running riot, and with her body behaving erratically, it was getting harder to keep her feelings under wraps. One thing she did know—she wanted her baby. As unplanned as it was, as challenging as it might be being a single mother, she had developed a strong and soul-reaching love for the child in her womb.

Family is everything...

It was. She knew that. She'd been raised by wonderful parents and loved her siblings dearly. Her baby would be enveloped in that love. She *could* go home, and Daniel need never know about her pregnancy. She'd considered it. Dreamed of it.

Except…

It would be wrong. Dishonest. And wholly unfair.

"I should very much like to visit your little town one day," Solana said cheerfully.

Crystal Point. It was a tiny seaside community of eight hundred people. From the pristine beaches to the rich soil of the surrounding farmlands, it would always be home, no matter where life took her.

"I'd like that, too," she said, and pushed her plate aside.

"Not hungry?" Solana asked, her keen light gray eyes watching everything she did.

Mary-Jayne shrugged. "Not really. But it is delicious," she said of the warm mango salad on her plate. "I'm not much use in the kitchen, so our lunches are always a nice change from the grilled-cheese sandwich I'd usually have."

Solana grinned. "Didn't your mother teach you to cook?"

"She tried, but I was something of a tomboy when I was young and more interested in helping my dad in his workshop," she explained.

"Well, those skills can come in handy, too."

Mary-Jayne nodded. "For sure. I can fix a leaking tap and build a bookcase…but a cheese toastie is about my limit in the kitchen."

"Well, you'll just have to find yourself a husband who can cook," Solana suggested, smiling broadly.

"I'm not really in the market for a husband." *Not since I got knocked up by your grandson…*

Solana smiled. "Nonsense. Everyone is looking for a soul mate…even a girl as independent and free-spirited as you."

Mary-Jayne nodded vaguely. Independent and free-spirited? It was exactly how she appeared to the world. And exactly how she liked it. But for the most part, it was a charade. A facade to fool everyone into thinking she had it all together—that she was strong and self-sufficient and happy-go-lucky. She'd left home at seventeen determined to prove she could make it on her own, and had spent ten years treading water in the hope no one noticed she was just getting by—both financially and emotionally. Her family loved her, no doubt about it. As the youngest child she was indulged and allowed to do whatever she liked, mostly without consequence. Her role as the lovable but unreliable flake in the Preston family had been set from a young age. While her older brother, Noah, took over the family business, perennial earth-mother Evie married young and pursued her art, and übersmart Grace headed for a career in New York before she returned to Australia to marry the man she loved.

But for Mary-Jayne there were no such expectations, and no traditional career. She'd gotten her first piercing at fourteen and had a tattoo by the time she was fifteen. When school was over she'd found a job as a cashier in a supermarket and a month later moved out of her parents' home and into a partly furnished cottage three streets away. She'd packed whatever she could fit into her battered Volkswagen and began her adult life away from the low expectations of her family. She never doubted their love... but sometimes she wished they expected more of her. Then perhaps she would have had more ambition, more focus.

Mary-Jayne pushed back her chair and stood up. "I'll take the dishes to the kitchen."

"Thank you. You're a sweet girl, Mary-Jayne," Solana said, and collected up the cutlery. "You know, I was just telling Caleb that very thing yesterday."

It was another not-so-subtle attempt to play match-maker.

Solana had somehow got it in her head that her younger grandson would be a good match for her. And the irony wasn't lost on Mary-Jayne. She liked Caleb. He was friendly and charming and came into the store every couple of days and asked how things were going, and always politely inquired after Audrey. The resort staff all respected him, and he clearly ran a tight ship.

But he didn't so much as cause a blip on her radar.

Unlike Daniel. He was the blip of the century.

Mary-Jayne ignored Solana's words, collected the dishes and headed for the kitchen. Once there she took a deep breath and settled her hips against the countertop. Her stomach was still queasy, and she took a few deep breaths before she turned toward the sink and decided to make a start on the dishes. She filled the sink and was about to plunge her hands into the water when she heard a decisive knock on the front door, and then seconds later the low sound of voices. Solana had a visitor. Mary-Jayne finished the washing up, dried her hands and headed for the door.

And then stopped in her tracks.

Even though his back was to her she recognized Daniel Anderson immediately. The dark chinos and white shirt fitted him as though they'd been specifically tailored for his broad, well-cut frame. She knew those shoulders and every other part of him because the memory of the night they'd spent together was etched into her brain, and the result was the child growing inside her.

Perhaps he'd tracked her down to confront her? Maybe he knew?

Impossible.

No one knew she was pregnant. It was a coincidence. He'd forgotten all about her. He hadn't called since she'd told him to go to hell. He'd returned to see his grand-mother. Mary-Jayne's hand moved to her belly, and she puffed out the smock-style shirt she wore. If she kept her arms to her sides and kept her clothing as loose as possible it was unlikely he'd notice her little baby bump. She lingered by the doorway, her mind racing at a trillion miles an hour.

Solana was clearly delighted to see him and hugged him twice in succession. "What a wonderful surprise," his grandmother said. "Why didn't you tell me you were coming?"

"Then it's not a surprise," he replied. "Is it?"

As they chatted Mary-Jayne moved back behind the architrave and considered her options. Come clean? Act nonchalant? Make a run for it? Running for it appealed most. This wasn't the time or place to make any kind of announcement about being pregnant, not with Solana in the room. She needed time to think. Prepare.

I have to get out of here.

The back door was through the kitchen and off the dining room. But if she sneaked out through the back Solana would want to know why. There would be questions. From Solana. And then from Daniel.

"Show some backbone," she muttered to herself.

She'd always had gumption. Now wasn't the time to ditch her usual resolve and act like a frightened little girl. Mary-Jayne was about to push back her shoulders and face the music when an unwelcome and unexpected wave of nausea rose up and made her suddenly forget everything else. She put a hand to her chest, heaved and swallowed hard, fighting the awful feeling with every ounce of willpower she possessed.

And failed.

She rushed forward to the closest exit, racing past Solana and *him* and headed across the room and out to the patio, just making it to the garden in time.

Where she threw up in spectacular and humiliating fashion.

Daniel remained where he was and watched as his grandmother hurried through the doorway and quickly attended to the still-vomiting woman who was bent over in the garden. If he thought he was needed Daniel would have helped, but he was pretty sure she would much prefer his grandmother coming to her aid.

After several minutes both women came back through the door. Mary-Jayne didn't look at him. Didn't even acknowledge he was there as she walked to the front door and let herself out, head bowed, arms rigid at her sides. But he was rattled seeing her. And silently cursed himself for having so little control over the effect she had on him.

"The poor thing," his grandmother said, hovering in the doorway before she finally closed the door. "She's been unwell for weeks. Ex-boyfriend trouble, too, I think. Not that she's said much to me about it…but I think there's been someone in the picture."

Boyfriend?

His gut twinged. "Does she need a doctor?" he asked, matter-of-fact.

"I don't think so," his grandmother replied. "Probably just a twenty-four-hour bug."

Daniel ignored the twitch of concern. Mary-Jayne had a way of making him feel a whole lot of things he didn't want or need. Attraction aside, she invaded his thoughts when he least expected it. She needled his subconscious. Like she had when he'd been on a date a couple of weeks back. He'd gone out with the tall leggy blonde he'd met at a business dinner, thinking she'd be a distraction. And spent the evening wishing he'd been with someone who would at least occasionally disagree and not be totally compliant to his whims. Someone like Mary-Jayne Preston. He'd ended up saying good-night to his date by nine o'clock, barely kissing her hand when he dropped her home. Sure, he didn't want a serious relationship, but he didn't want boring conversation and shallow sex, either.

And since there had been nothing boring or shallow about the night he'd spent with the bewitching brunette, Daniel still wanted her in his bed. Despite his good sense telling him otherwise.

"So," Solana said, and raised her hands. "Why have you come home?"

"To see you. Why else?"

She tutted. "Always a question with a question. Even as a toddler you were inquisitive. Always questioning everything, always asking *why* to your grandfather. Your brothers were never as curious about things as you were. Do you remember when you were eight and persuaded your grandfather to let you ride that mad, one-eyed pony your dad saved from the animal rescue center?" She shook her head and grinned. "Everyone wanted to know why you'd want to get on such a crazy animal. And all you said was, *why not?*"

Daniel shrugged. "As I recall I dislocated my collarbone."

"And scared Bernie and me half to death," Solana said and chuckled. "You were a handful, you know. Always getting into scraps. Always pushing the envelope. Amazing you turned out so sensible."

"Who say's I'm sensible?" he inquired lightly.

Solana's smile widened. "Me. Your brothers. Your grandfather if he was still alive."

"And Miles?"

His grandmother raised a silvery brow. "I think your dad would like you to be a little *less* sensible."

"I think my father would like me to eat tofu and drive a car that runs on doughnut grease."

"My son is who he is," Solana said affectionately. "Your grandfather never understood Miles and his alternative ways. But your dad knows who he is and what he wants from life. *And* he knows how to relax and enjoy the simple things."

Daniel didn't miss the dig. It wasn't the first time he'd been accused of being an uptight killjoy by his family. "I can relax."

His grandmother looked skeptical. "Well, perhaps you can learn to while you're here."

Daniel crossed his arms. Something about her tone made him suspicious. "You knew I was coming?"

Solana nodded, clearly unapologetic. "Blake called me. And of course it was my idea." She sat down at the table. "Did you know your grandfather had his first heart attack at thirty-nine?"

Daniel sighed. He'd heard it before. Mike Anderson died at sixty-nine from a massive coronary. His fourth. After two previous bypass surgeries the final heart attack had been swift and fatal, killing him before he'd had a chance to get up from his desk. "Gran, I—"

"Don't fob me off with some vague assurance that it won't happen to you," she said, cutting him off. "You work too hard. You don't take time off. You've become as defined by Anderson Holdings as your grandfather was... and all it got him was an early grave. There's more to life than business."

He would have dismissed the criticism from anyone else...but not Solana. He loved and respected his grandmother, and her opinion was one of the few that mattered to him.

"I know that. But I'm not ready to—"

"It's been over four years," Solana reminded him gently. "And time you got back to the land of the living. Simone wouldn't want you to—"

"Gran," Daniel said, hanging on to his patience. "I know you're trying to help. And I promise I'll relax and unwind while I'm here. I'm back for a week so I'll—"

"You'll need more than a week to unwind," she said, cutting him off again. "But if that's all you can manage then so be it. And your parents are expecting you to visit, in case you were thinking you'd fly under the radar while you're here."

Guilt spiked between his shoulder blades. Solana had a way of doing that. And he hadn't considered *not* seeing his father and stepmother. Not really. True, he had little in common with Miles and Bernadette…but they *were* his parents, and he knew they'd be genuinely pleased that he'd come home for a visit.

From a young age he'd known where his path lay. He was who his grandfather looked to as his protégé. At eighteen he'd been drafted into Anderson's, studying economics at night school so he could learn the business firsthand from his grandfather. At twenty-three, following Mike Anderson's death, he'd taken over the reins and since then he'd lived and breathed Anderson's. Blake and Caleb had followed him a few years later, while Daniel remained at the helm.

He worked and had little time for anything resembling a personal life. Simone had understood that. She was a corporate lawyer and worked seventy-hour weeks. Marrying her had made sense. They were a good match…alike in many ways, and they'd been happy together. And would still be together if fate and a faulty brake line hadn't intervened. She'd still be a lawyer and he would still spend his waking hours living and breathing Anderson Holdings. And they would be parents to their daughter. Just as they'd planned.

Daniel stretched his shoulders and stifled a yawn. He was tired. Jet-lagged. But if he crashed in the afternoon he'd feel worse. The trick to staying on top of the jet lag was keeping normal sleep patterns. Besides, there were two things he wanted to do—take a shower, and see Mary-Jayne Preston.

Mary-Jayne knew that the knock on her door would be Daniel. She'd been waiting for the sound for the past hour. But the sharp rap still startled her and she jumped up from the sofa, where she'd been sitting, hands twisted and stomach churning.

She walked across the living room and down the short hallway, grappling with the emotions running riot throughout her. She ruffled out her baggy shirt and hoped it disguised her belly enough to give her some time to work out how she was going to tell the man at her door he was going to become a father. She took a deep breath, steadied her knees, grabbed the handle and opened the door.

His gray eyes immediately looked her over with unconcealed interest. "How are you feeling?"

His lovely accent wound up her spine. "Fine."

"My grandmother is worried about you."

"I'm fine, like I said."

He tilted his head slightly. "You sure about that?"

Her chin came up. "Positive. Not that I have to explain myself to you."

"No," he mused. "I guess you don't."

"Is there something else you wanted?"

A tiny smile creased one corner of his mouth. "Can I come in?"

"I'd rather you didn't," she said, and stepped back, shielding herself behind the door. "But since you own this resort I guess you can do whatever the hell you want."

There was laughter in his eyes, and she realized the more hostile she got, the more amused he appeared. Mary-Jayne took a deep breath and turned on her heels, quickly finding solace behind the single recliner chair just a few feet away. She watched as he closed the door and took a few easy strides into the room.

"I hear you've been taking my grandmother to see fortune-tellers?"

Solana had told him about that? The older woman had sworn her to secrecy, saying her grandsons would think her crazy for visiting a clairvoyant. "It was *one* fortune-teller," she informed him. "And a reputable one, I might add."

His brows came up. "Really? You believe in all that nonsense?"

She glared at him. "Well, she did say I'd meet a man who was a real jerk...so I'd say she was pretty accurate, wouldn't you agree?"

"Is that a question?" he shot back. "Because I'm probably not the best judge of my own character. Other people's characters, on the other hand, I can usually peg."

"Don't start with—"

"Why did you hang up on me when I called you?"

She was genuinely surprised by his question. And didn't respond.

"You were in South Dakota at your friend's wedding," he reminded her. "I was in San Francisco. I would have flown you to the city."

Into the city. And into his bed. Mary-Jayne knew the score. She might have been a fool the night of Solana's birthday party, but she certainly wasn't about to repeat that monumental mistake.

"I wasn't in the market for another meaningless one-night stand."

His mouth twitched. "Really? More to the point, I guess your boyfriend wouldn't have approved?"

She frowned. "My what?"

"My grandmother can be indiscreet," he said and looked her over. "Unintentionally of course, since she has no idea we had that *meaningless one-night stand.*"

Color rose and spotted her cheeks. And for several long seconds she felt a kind of riveting connection to him. It was illogical. It was relentless. It made it impossible to ignore him. Or forget the night they'd spent together. Or the way they'd made love. The silence stretched between them, and Mary-Jayne was drawn deep into his smoky gray eyes.

"I don't have a boyfriend or lover," she said quietly. "I made that up to stop Solana from asking questions about..." Her words trailed off and she moved back, putting distance between them.

"About what?"

She shook her head. "Nothing. I really can't... I can't do this."

"Do what?" he asked.

"I can't do this with you."

"We're not doing anything," he said. "Just talking."

"That's just it," she said, her voice coming out a little strangled. "I'm not ready for this. Not here. Not today. I feel unwell and I—"

"I thought you said you were feeling better?" he asked, cutting her off.

"Well, I'm not, okay? I'm not better. And seeing you here only makes me feel worse."

"Such brutal honesty. I don't know whether to be flattered or offended."

She let out an agonized moan. "That's just it. I am honest. *Always*. And seeing you now makes it impossible for me to be anything else. And I'm not ready for it... I can't do this today. I simply can't—"

"What are you talking about?" he asked impatiently and cut her off again.

"I'm talking about... I mean... I can't..."

"Mary-Jayne," he said, saying her name like he had that night, when he'd said it over and over, against her skin, against her breath. "I'm not sure what's going on with you, but you're not making much sense."

The truth screamed to be told. There was no other way. She couldn't stop being who she was. She was an honest, forthright person who wore her heart on her sleeve. Mary-Jayne stepped out from behind the chair and spread her hands across her stomach, tightening the baggy shirt over her middle. Highlighting the small bump that hadn't been there four months ago.

"I'm talking about *this*."

Daniel quickly refocused his gaze onto her middle and frowned. "You're pregnant?"

She nodded and swallowed hard. "Yes."

"And?"

She shrugged and her hair flipped around her shoulders. Now or never.

"And isn't it obvious? You're the father."

Chapter Three

He hadn't moved. Mary-Jayne looked at him and took a long breath. "This isn't how I wanted you to find out. I was going to call and tell you and—"

"You're not serious?" he asked, cutting through her words with icy precision.

She nodded. "I'm perfectly serious. I'm pregnant."

He raised a dark brow. "We used protection," he said quietly and held up a few fingers. "Three times, three lots of birth control. So your math doesn't quite work out."

"My math?" She stared at him. "What exactly are you accusing me of?"

"Nothing," he replied evenly. "Simply stating an irrefutable fact."

A fact?

Right. There was no possible way of misunderstanding his meaning. "I'm not lying to you. This baby is—"

"Yours," he corrected coldly. "And probably the ex-boyfriend who my grandmother said is giving you grief at the moment."

She fought the urge to rush across the room and slug him. "I don't have a *boyfriend*. Ex or otherwise."

"You do according to my grandmother," he stated. "Who I trust more than anyone else."

No punches pulled. He didn't believe her. *Okay.* She could handle it. She didn't care what he thought. "I only told Solana that to stop her from asking questions about why I've been unwell."

He crossed his arms, accentuating his broad shoulders, and stood as still as a statue. He really was absurdly good-looking, she thought, disliking him with every fiber in her body. His gray eyes had darkened to a deep slate color and his almost black hair was short and shiny, and she remembered how soft it had been between her fingertips. His face was perfectly proportioned and he had a small cleft in his chin that was ridiculously sexy. Yes, Daniel Anderson was as handsome as sin. He was also an arrogant, overbearing, condescending so-and-so, and if it weren't for the fact he was the biological father of her child, she'd happily *never* see him again.

"Do I really appear so gullible, Miss Preston?"

Miss Preston?

"Gullible? I don't know what you—"

"If you think naming me in a paternity claim will fatten your bank balance, think again. My lawyers will be all over you in a microsecond."

His pompous arrogance was unbelievable. "I'm not after your money."

"Then, what?" he asked. "A wedding ring?"

Fury surged through her. "I wouldn't marry you if you were the last man left on the planet."

Her words seemed to amuse him and he looked at her

in such a haughty, condescending way that her palms actually itched with the urge to slap his face. In every way she'd played the scene out in her head, and not once had she imagined he wouldn't believe that her baby was his. Naive perhaps, but Mary-Jayne had been raised to take someone at their word.

"That's quite a relief, since I won't be proposing anytime soon."

"Go to hell," she said quietly as emotion tightened her chest, and she drew in a shuddering breath. He pushed her buttons effortlessly. He really was a hateful jerk.

"Not until we've sorted out this little mix-up."

"Mix-up?" She glared at him. "I'm pregnant and you're the father. This is not a mix-up. This is just how it is."

"Then, I demand a paternity test."

Daniel hadn't meant to sound like such a cold, unfeeling bastard. But he wasn't about to be taken for a ride. He knew the score. A few months back his brother Caleb had been put through the ringer in a paternity suit that had eventually proved the kid he'd believed was his wasn't. And Daniel wasn't about to get pulled into that same kind of circus.

Mary-Jayne Preston's baby couldn't possibly be his… could it? He'd never played roulette with birth control. Besides, now that he could well and truly see her baby bump she looked further along than four months. Simone hadn't started showing so obviously until she was five months' pregnant.

"I'd like you to leave."

Daniel didn't move. "Won't that defeat the purpose of your revelation?"

She scowled, and he couldn't help thinking how she still looked beautiful even with an infuriated expression.

"You know about the baby, so whatever you decide to do with the information is up to you."

"Until I get served with child-support demands, you mean?"

She placed her hands on her hips and Daniel's gaze was immediately drawn to her belly. She was rounder than he remembered, kind of voluptuous, and a swift niggle of attraction wound its way through his blood and across his skin. Her curves had appealed to him from the moment they'd first met, and watching her now only amplified that desire.

Which was damned inconvenient, since she was obviously trying to scam him.

"I don't want your money," she said stiffly. "And I certainly don't want a wedding ring. When I get married it will be to someone I actually like. I intend to raise this baby alone. Believe me, or don't believe me. Frankly, I don't care either way."

There was such blatant contempt in her voice that he was tempted to smile. One thing about the woman in front of him—she wasn't afraid to speak her mind. And even though he knew it was crazy thinking, it was an interesting change from the usual lengths some women went to in order to get his attention. How sincere she was, he couldn't tell.

"We spent the night together a little over four months ago," he reminded her. "You look more than four months pregnant."

Her glare intensified. "So it's clearly a big baby. All I know is that the only possible way I got pregnant was from that night I spent with you. I hadn't been with anyone for a long time before that night. Despite what you think of me, I'm not easy. And I don't lie. I have no reason to want this child to be yours. I don't like you. I'm not interested in you or your money or anything else. But I am telling you the truth."

He still wasn't convinced. "So the ex-boyfriend?"

"A figment of my imagination," she replied. "Like I said, Solana was asking questions and I needed a little camouflage for a while."

He kept his head. "Even if there is no boyfriend and you are indeed carrying a supersize baby...we used contraception. So it doesn't add up."

"And since condoms are only ninety-eight percent effective, we obviously managed to slip into the two percent bracket."

Ninety-eight percent effective?

Since when?

Daniel struggled with the unease clawing up his spine. "You cannot expect me to simply accept this news at face value."

She shrugged, as if she couldn't care either way. "Do, or don't. If you want a paternity test to confirm it, then fine, that's what we'll do."

He relaxed a little. Finally, some good sense. "Thank you."

"But it won't be done until the baby is born," she said evenly and took a long breath. "There are risks associated with tests after the fifteen-week mark, and I won't put my baby in jeopardy. Not for you. Not for anyone."

There was such unequivocal resolve in her voice, and it surprised him. She was a flake. Unreliable. Unpredictable. Nothing like Simone. "Of course," he said, and did his best to ignore the stabbing pain in his temple. His shoulders ached, and he could feel the effects of no sleep and hours flying across the globe begin to creep into his limbs. "I wouldn't expect you to put your child at risk."

Her child.

Her baby.

This wasn't what he'd expected to face when he'd decided to come home. But if she was telling the truth? What then? To share a child with a woman he barely knew. It was a train wreck waiting to happen.

And he hated waiting. In business. In his personal life.

He'd waited at the hospital when Simone was brought in with critical injuries. He waited while the doctors had tried to save her and their unborn daughter. He'd waited, and then received the worst possible news. And afterward he'd experienced a heartbreaking despair. After that night he became hollow inside. He'd loved his wife and daughter. Losing them had been unbearable. And he'd never wanted to feel that kind of soul-destroying anguish again.

But if Mary-Jayne *was* carrying his child, how could he turn his back?

He couldn't. He'd be trapped.

Held ransom by the very feelings he'd sworn he never wanted to feel again.

"So what do you want from me until then?"

"Want? Nothing," she replied quietly. "I'll call you when the baby is born and the paternity test is done. Goodbye."

He sighed. "Is this how you usually handle problems? By ignoring them?"

Her cheeks quickly heated. "I don't consider this baby a problem," she shot back. "And the only thing I plan to ignore is you."

He stared at her for a moment, and then when he laughed Mary-Jayne realized she liked the sound way too much. She didn't want to like *anything* about him. Not ever. He had become enemy number one. For the next five months all she wanted to do was concentrate on growing a healthy baby. Wasting time thinking about Daniel and his sexy laugh and gray eyes was off her agenda.

"You don't really think that's going to happen, do you?" he asked, watching her with such hot intensity she couldn't look away. "You've dropped this bombshell, and you know enough about me to realize I won't simply fade away for the next five months."

"I can live in hope."

"I think you live in a fantasyland, Mary-Jayne."

The way he said her name caused her skin to prickle. No one called her that except her parents and her older brother, Noah. Even her sisters and closest friends mostly called her M.J. To the rest of the world she was M. J. Preston—the youngest and much loved sibling in a close-knit middle-class family. But Daniel had always used her full name.

Mary-Jayne took a deep breath. "A fantasyland?" She repeated his words as a question.

"What else would you call it?" he shot back as he looked her over. "You're what, twenty-seven? Never married or engaged. No real career to speak of. And a barely solvent online business. You've rented the same house for nearly ten years. You drive a car that's good for little else but scrap metal. You have less than a thousand dollars in the bank at any given time and a not-so-stellar credit rating thanks to a certain dubious ex-boyfriend who ran up a debt on your behalf over five years ago. It looks very much like you do—"

"How do you know that?" she demanded hotly, hands on hips. "How do you know all that about me? I've not told Solana any of..." She trailed off as realization hit. And then she seethed. "You had me investigated?"

"Of course," he replied, unmoving and clearly unapologetic.

"You had no right to do that," she spat. "No right at all. You invaded my privacy."

He shrugged his magnificent shoulders. "You are working at this resort and have befriended my grandmother—it was prudent to make sure you weren't a fortune hunter."

"Fortune hunter?" Mary-Jayne's eyes bulged wide and she said a rude word.

He tilted his head a fraction. "Well, the jury's still out on that one."

"Jury?" She echoed the word in disbelief. "And what does that make you? The judge? Can you actually hear yourself? Of all the pompous, arrogant and self-important things I've ever heard in my life, you take the cake. And you really do take yourself and the significance of your opinions way too seriously."

He didn't like that. Not one bit. She watched, fascinated as his eyes darkened and a tiny pulse in his cheek beat rapidly. His hands were clenched and suddenly his body looked as if it had been carved from granite. And as much as she tried to fight it, attraction reared up, and heat swirled around the small room as their gazes clashed.

Memories of that night four months ago banged around in her head. Kissing, touching, stroking. Possession and desire unlike any she had known before. There had been a quiet intensity in him that night, and she'd been swept away into another world, another universe where only pleasure and a deeply intimate connection existed. That night, he hadn't been the rigid, unyielding and disagreeable man who was now in her living room. He'd been tender and passionate. He'd whispered her name against her skin. He'd kissed her and made love to her with such profound eagerness Mary-Jayne's entire mind and body had awakened and responded in kind. She'd never been driven to please and be pleasured like that before.

But right now she had to get back to hating him. "I'm going to get changed and go for a walk to clear my head. You know the way out."

He didn't move. And he looked a little pale, she thought. Perhaps the shock that he was going to be a father was finally hitting home. But then she remembered that he didn't believe he actually was her baby's father, so that probably wasn't it.

"We still have things to discuss."

"Not for another…" Her words trailed off and she tapped off five of her fingers in her palm. "Five months. Until then, how about you treat me with the disdain that you've clearly mastered, and I'll simply pretend that you don't exist. That will work out nicely for us both, don't you think?"

Of course, she knew saying something so provocative was like waving a red cape at a bull. But she couldn't help herself. He deserved it in spades. And it was only the truth. She didn't want to see him or spend any more time in his company.

"I don't treat you with disdain."

And there it was again—his resolute belief in the sound of his own voice.

"No?" She bit down on her lip for a moment. "You've admitted you had me investigated and just accused me of being a fortune hunter. Oh, and what about what you said to me on the phone when I was in South Dakota?" She took a strengthening breath. "That I was a flake who dressed like a hippie."

His eyes flashed. "And before you told me to go to hell you called me an uptight, overachieving, supercilious snob, if I remember correctly." He uncrossed his arms and took a step toward her.

"Well, it's the truth. You are an uptight snob."

"And you dress like a hippie."

"I like to be comfortable," she said, and touched her head self-consciously. "And I can't help the way my hair gets all curly in the humidity."

His gaze flicked to her hair and she saw his mouth twitch fractionally. "I didn't say a word about your hair. In fact it's quite…it's…it's…"

"It's what?" she asked.

"Nothing," he said, and shrugged. "I would like to know your plans."

Mary-Jayne stared at him. "I don't have any plans other than to have a healthy baby in five months' time."

He looked around the room. "When are you leaving here?"

"Audrey's back in two weeks. I'll go home then."

"Have you told your family?"

She shook her head. "Not yet."

"Have you told anyone?"

She met his gaze. "You."

His expression narrowed. "And since she didn't mention it while you were throwing up in her garden, I'm guessing you haven't told my grandmother, either?"

"Just you," she replied, fighting the resentment fueling her blood. "Like I said. Incidentally, Daniel, if you're going to disbelieve everything that comes out of my mouth, it's going to be a long five months."

He grinned unexpectedly. "So you do know my name? I don't think you've ever used it before. Well, except for that night we spent together."

Her skin heated. She remembered exactly how she'd said his name that night. Over and over, whispered and moaned, as though it was the only word she'd known.

"Like I said, you know the way out."

He didn't budge. "We still need to talk."

"We've talked enough," she said tensely. "You don't believe me and you need a paternity test. *And* you think I'm after your money. Believe me, I've got your message loud and clear."

"You're angry because I want proof of paternity?"

He actually sounded surprised. Mary-Jayne almost laughed at his absurd sense of entitlement. "I'm angry because you think I'm lying to you. I don't know what kind of world you live in where you have this compulsion to question someone's integrity without cause, but I don't live in that world, Daniel. And I would never want to."

She spun on her heel and left the room, barely taking a breath until she reached the sanctuary of the main bedroom. She leaned against the closed door and shuddered.

It's done now. He knows. I can get on with things.

She pulled herself together, changed into sweats and sneakers and loitered in the room for more than ten minutes to ensure he'd be gone.

She strode into the living room and then stopped in her tracks. The room was empty. He'd left. As if he'd never been there.

A strange hollowness fluttered behind her ribs. She was glad he was gone—arrogant and disbelieving jerk that he was. She was well rid of him. With any luck she'd never have to see him again. Or speak to him. Or have to stare into those smoky gray eyes of his.

She could go home and have her baby.

Simple.

But in her heart she knew she was dreaming to believe he'd just disappear from her life. She was having his baby—and that made it about as complicated as it got.

When Daniel woke up he had a crick in his neck and his left leg was numb. It was dark out. He checked his watch: six-forty. He sat up and stretched. When he'd left her condo, he'd walked around the grounds for a few minutes before heading back to his own villa. Once he'd sat down, the jet lag had hit him with a thud. Now he needed coffee and a clear head.

He got to his feet and rounded out his shoulders. The condo was quiet, and he walked from the living room and headed for the kitchen. He had to refocus and figure what the hell he was supposed to do for the next five months until the baby came into the world.

The baby.

His baby...

I'm going to be a father.

Maybe?

Daniel still wasn't entirely convinced. Mary-Jayne potentially had a lot to gain by saying he'd fathered her child. He wasn't naive and knew some people were mercenary enough to try to take advantage of others. He remembered how devastated Caleb had been when he'd discovered the boy he'd thought was his son turned out to belong to his *then* girlfriend's ex-husband. And Daniel didn't want to form a bond with a child only to have it snatched away. Not again. Losing Simone and their unborn daughter had been soul destroying. He wasn't going to put himself in a position to get another serving of that kind of loss.

He made coffee and drank it. Damn...he felt as if his head was going to explode. He'd had it all planned out... come back to Port Douglas, reconnect with Mary-Jayne for a week and get her out of his system once and for all.

Not going to happen.

Daniel rounded out his shoulders and sucked in a long breath. He needed a plan. And fast. He swilled the cup in the sink, grabbed his keys and left the villa.

By the time he reached her condo his hands were sweating. No one had ever had such an intense physical effect on him. And he wasn't sure how to feel about it. The crazy thing was, he couldn't ignore it. And now that had amplified a hundredfold.

They needed to talk. There was no way around it. Daniel took another breath and knocked on the door.

When she answered the door she looked almost as though she'd been expecting him to return. He didn't like the idea that he was so transparent to her.

"I'm working," she said, and left him standing in the doorway. "So you'll need to amuse yourself for ten minutes before we get into round two."

The way she dismissed him so effortlessly *should* have made him madder than hell. But it didn't. He liked her spirit, and it was one of the things he found so attractive about her.

He followed her down the hall, and when he reached the dining room she was already standing by a small workbench tucked against the wall in one corner. She was bent over the narrow table, one elbow resting, using a small soldering iron. There was enough light from the lamp positioned to one side for him to see her profile, and despite the protective glasses perched on her nose he couldn't miss the intense concentration she gave her craft. There were several boards fashioned on easels that displayed her jewelry pieces, and although he was no expert, there was certainly style and creativity in her work.

She must have sensed him watching her because she turned and switched off the soldering iron. "So you're back?"

He nodded. "I'm back."

"Did you call your lawyer?"

"What?"

She shrugged a little. "Seems like something you'd do."

Daniel ignored the irritation clawing at his spine. "No, Mary-Jayne, I didn't call my lawyer. Actually, I fell asleep."

She looked surprised and then frowned a little. "Jet lag?"

He nodded again. "Once I sat down it hit me."

"I had the same reaction when I returned from Thailand last year. It took me three days to recover. The trick is to stay awake until bedtime."

There was something husky and incredibly sexy about Mary-Jayne's voice that reached him deep down. After they'd slept together, he'd pursued her and she'd turned him down flat. Even from across an ocean she'd managed to throw a bucket of cold water on his attempts to ask her out. And get her back in his bed. Because he still wanted her. As foolish as it was, as different and unsuitable for one another as they were—he couldn't stop thinking about her.

She knew that. She knew they were from different worlds. She'd accused him of thinking she was an easy mark and that was why he wanted her. But it wasn't that. He wanted her because she stirred him like no other woman ever had. From her crazy beautiful hair to her curvy body and her sassy mouth, Daniel had never known a woman like her. He might not like her...but he wanted her. And it was as inconvenient as hell.

"So what do you want, then?"

Daniel's back straightened. She didn't hold back. She clearly didn't think she had anything to gain by being friendly or even civil. It wasn't a tactic he was used to. She'd called him a spoiled, pampered and arrogant snob, and although he didn't agree with that assumption, it was exactly how she treated him.

"To talk," he replied. "Seems we've got plenty to talk about."

"Do you think?" she shot back. "Since you don't believe

that this baby is yours, I can't see what's so important that you felt compelled to come back so soon."

Daniel took a breath. "I guess I deserve that."

"Yeah," she said and plucked the glasses off her nose. "I guess you do."

He managed a tight smile. "I would like to talk with you. Would coffee be too much trouble?"

She placed the soldering iron on the bench. "I guess not."

As she walked past him and through the door to the kitchen it occurred to Daniel that she swayed when she moved. The kitchen seemed small with both of them in it, and he stayed on the outside of the counter.

"That's quite a collection your friend has up there," he remarked and pointed to the cooking pots hanging from an old window shutter frame that was suspended from the ceiling.

"Audrey likes pans," she said without looking at him. "I don't know why."

"She doesn't need a reason," he said and pulled out a chair. "I collect old books."

She glanced up. "Old books?"

"First editions," he explained. "Poetry and classic literature."

One of her eyebrows rose subtly. "I didn't peg you as a reader. Except perhaps the *Financial Times*."

Daniel grinned a little. "I didn't say I read them."

"Then why collect them?"

He half shrugged. "They're often unique. You know, rare."

"Valuable?" she asked, saying the word almost as an insult. "Does everything in your life have a dollar sign attached to it?"

Guilt niggled its way through his blood. "I appreciate you agreeing to a paternity test."

She shrugged lightly. "There's little point in being at odds over this. Be assured that I don't want anything from you, and once you have your proof of paternity you can decide how much or how little time you invest in this."

As she spoke she certainly didn't come across as flighty as she appeared. She sounded like a woman who knew exactly what she wanted. Which was her child...and no interference from him.

Which of course wasn't going to happen.

If the baby *was* his, then he would be very involved. He'd have no choice. The child would be an Anderson and have the right to claim the legacy that went with the name. Only, he wasn't sure how he'd get Mary-Jayne to see it that way.

"If this child is mine, then I won't dodge my responsibility."

She looked less than impressed by the idea. "If you're talking about money, I think I've made it pretty clear I'm not interested."

"You can't raise a child on good intentions, Mary-Jayne. Be sensible."

Her mouth thinned and she looked ready for an argument, but she seemed to change her mind. Some battles, he figured, were about defense, not attack...and she knew that as well as he did.

"We'll see what happens," she said casually as she crossed the small kitchen and stood in front of the refrigerator. She waited for him to stand aside and then opened the door. "I'm heating up lasagna. Are you staying for dinner?"

Daniel raised a brow. "Am I invited?"

She shrugged, as if she couldn't care either way. But

he knew she probably wanted to tell him to take a hike in some of her more colorful language.

"Sure," he said, and grabbed the coffee mug as he stepped out of her way. "That would be good."

He caught a tiny smile on her mouth and watched as she removed several items from the refrigerator and began preparing food on the countertop. She placed a casserole dish in the microwave and began making a salad. And Daniel couldn't take his eyes off her. She was fascinating to watch. Her glorious hair shone like ebony beneath the kitchen light, and she chewed her bottom lip as she completed the task. And of course thinking about her lips made him remember their night together. And kissing her. And making love to her. She had a remarkable effect on his libido, and he wondered if it was because they *were* so different that he was so achingly attracted to her. She was all challenge. All resistance. And since very little challenged him these days, Daniel knew her very determination to avoid him had a magnetic pull all of its own.

And he had no idea what he was going to do about it.

Or if he could do actually do anything at all.

Chapter Four

Mary-Jayne finished preparing dinner, uncomfortably conscious of the gorgeous man standing by the kitchen table. There was such blistering intensity in his gaze she could barely concentrate on what she was doing. She hated that he could do that to her. If she had her way she'd never see him again.

But the baby she carried bound them together.

He wouldn't, she was certain, simply disappear from her life.

She had five months until the baby came, and she had to figure out how to get through those months with Daniel in the background. Or worse. He wasn't the kind of man who'd simply go away until the baby came…regardless of how much she might wish for things to go that way.

"How long are you staying at the resort?" she asked, hoping he'd say not too long at all. Best he leave quickly.

"I'd planned to only be here a week to visit with my

grandmother," he replied, and shrugged slightly. "But now I'm not sure."

She frowned. "Don't you have a company to run or something?"

"Yes."

"Isn't it hard to do that from here? You live mostly in San Francisco, right?"

He placed the mug on the dining table and crossed his arms. "Most of the time. Anderson's corporate offices are there. And the Bay Area resort is the largest."

"Well, I'm sure they need you back."

His mouth twitched. "Eager to see me gone, Mary-Jayne?"

"If I said no I'd be lying," she replied, and brought plates and cutlery to the table. "And as I've repeatedly said, I don't lie. So if you're thinking of extending your stay on my account, there's really no need. The birth is five months away and there's nothing you can do until then."

Mary-Jayne brought the food to the table and gestured for him to take a seat. When he was sitting she did the same and took the lids off the salad and lasagna. She didn't bother to ask what he wanted and quickly piled a scoop of pasta on his plate. Once she'd filled her own plate she picked up the utensils and speared some lettuce and cucumber with a fork.

"What...is...that?"

She looked up and smirked when she saw how Daniel was staring at his food. "Lasagna. With mushroom, spinach, shredded zucchini flowers and goat cheese."

He looked as if she'd asked him to chew broken glass. He took a breath and met her gaze. "You're a vegetarian?"

"Of course."

Mary-Jayne knew his parents were strict vegans. She

also knew he and his brothers had made a point from his early teens of *not* following in their footsteps.

"Of course," he repeated with more than a touch of irony. "Looks…delicious."

"I'm not much of a cook," she said frankly. "So don't hold your breath."

"Thanks for the warning."

She smiled to herself as they began to eat. He was being good-humored about her attempts to wind him up and it surprised her. Maybe he wasn't quite as straitlaced and uptight as she'd believed. Which didn't mean anything. He could be nice. He could be the most charming and agreeable man on the planet and it wouldn't change the one significant fact—they were like oil and water and would never mix. Despite the fact that they'd made a baby together and were now bound by parenthood. They were in different leagues, and she had to remember that every time she was tempted to think about his sexy voice and broad shoulders.

"I have an ultrasound appointment on Tuesday at ten-thirty," she said, and speared some pasta. "My doctor gave me a referral to a medical center in Cairns."

The regional city was forty miles south of Port Douglas.

"And?"

"And you're welcome to come along if you want to," she replied flatly.

He didn't really look as though he wanted to. But he did nod. "I'll pick you up."

"I can drive myself."

He raised a brow. "I'll pick you up."

She was about to argue, but stopped herself. Battling with Daniel over the small stuff was pointless. "Okay," she said, and didn't miss the flash of surprise in his eyes.

For a while the only sound in the room was the clicking of cutlery. He seemed happy not to talk and Mary-Jayne was content to eat her food and not think about how intimate the situation was. Once dinner was done he offered to help wash up, and before she had a chance to refuse his assistance he was out of the chair and in the kitchen, rinsing the plates with one hand while he opened the dishwasher with the other.

"You know your way around a kitchen," she said, surprised.

He shrugged. "Bernie made sure my brothers and I knew how to cook and clean up."

"That's your mother?"

"Stepmother," he replied, and began stacking the dishwasher. "She married my dad when I was two."

Her insides contracted. "Solana told me your mother passed away just after you were born."

"That's right."

Mary-Jayne moved into the kitchen. "You were born in Australia, weren't you?"

"That's right. My dad moved to California when he married Bernie and the twins were born there. They moved back here about ten years ago."

"I like your dad."

He glanced sideways. "I didn't realize you were acquainted."

"He came here to visit your grandmother and Caleb a few weeks ago. I was with Solana at the time and she introduced me to him. He had a very relaxed sense of self, if that makes sense. He was very charismatic and friendly," she said, and smiled a little.

"Not like me, you mean?"

Mary-Jayne grabbed a tea towel. "I'm sure you could be the same if you put your mind to it."

He turned and faced her. "And ruin my image of being an uptight bore?"

She laughed softly. "One thing you're not, Daniel, is boring."

"Just uptight?" he asked.

Mary-Jayne shrugged lightly. "I guess it goes with the territory. Solana told me how you took over the business when you were in your early twenties. That must have been quite a responsibility to shoulder. Duty above all else, right?"

He didn't move. "My grandfather was dead. My father had tried his hand at the business and bailed when he realized he was happier growing organic vegetables and pursuing his art. So yes, being drafted into the business that young had its challenges. But I wasn't about to let my family down. Or the people who rely on Anderson's for their livelihood. I did what I had to do... If that made me an uptight bore in the process, then I guess I'll simply have to live with it."

She took a deep breath. There was something so seductive about his deep voice it was impossible to move. She could have easily moved closer to him. The heat that had been between them from the start was as vibrant and scorching as it had ever been.

It's just sex...

Of course she knew that. Sex and lust and some kind of manic chemical reaction that had her hormones running riot. She had to get them under control. And fast.

"So I'll see you Tuesday. Around nine o'clock."

His gaze darkened. "Are you kicking me out?"

Mary-Jayne took a tentative step backward. "I guess so."

He laughed. "You know, I've never met anyone quite like you. There are no punches pulled with you, Mary-Jayne— you say exactly what you think."

"Blame it on my middle-class upbringing."

"I'm not criticizing you," he said, and folded his arms. "On the contrary, I find it intriguing. And incredibly sexy."

She stepped back again. "If you're flirting with me, stop right now. Your *charm* has got us into enough trouble already."

He laughed again. "Good night, Mary-Jayne."

"Good night," she whispered as she followed him up the hall, and she didn't take a breath until she closed the front door behind him.

After a restless night spent staring mostly at the ceiling, Daniel went for a long run along the beach around ten o'clock on Sunday morning. He stayed out for over an hour, and when he returned to his villa, took a shower and dressed and was about to head for his grandmother's when there was a tap on his door.

It was Caleb.

His brother walked across the threshold and dropped a set of keys onto the narrow hall table. "The keys to my Jeep," Caleb said and grinned. "In case you want to visit the folks."

Caleb never failed to remind him or Blake about the importance of family.

"Thanks," he said, and walked down the hallway.

His brother followed, and they each dropped into one of the two leather sofas in the living room. "Have you heard from Audrey?" Daniel asked the one question he knew his brother wouldn't want to answer.

Caleb shook his head. "I screwed up, and she's not about to forgive me anytime soon."

"You did what you thought was right."

"I moved my ex-girlfriend and her child into my house without thinking about what it would mean to my *current* girlfriend. I mean, I know Audrey and I had only been together a couple of months…but still…" The regretful look on his brother's face spoke volumes. "I should have done things differently. I shouldn't have taken Nikki's word that he was my kid without getting tested. I should have known Audrey was going to end up bailing. Hell, I probably would have done the same thing had the situation been reversed. When her mother got sick she had just the out she needed to get away from the resort for a while…and from me."

Which had been the catalyst for Mary-Jayne coming to the resort. Daniel was certain that his brother was in love with Mary-Jayne's friend Audrey. But when his ex-girlfriend had arrived on his doorstep, holding a baby she'd claimed was his, Caleb had reacted instinctively and moved them into his home.

"She's coming back in two weeks."

"Audrey?" Caleb's gaze narrowed. "How do you know that?"

He shrugged. "Gran must have mentioned it."

"Gran did?" His brother raised both brows. "You sure about that?"

"I don't know what—"

"Less than twenty-four hours, hey?" Caleb laughed. "I take it you've seen her?"

Her.

He'd told Caleb about spending the night with Mary-Jayne. He hadn't been able to avoid it since his brother had spotted her leaving his villa early that morning. "Yes, I've seen her."

"You still hung up on her?"

Daniel shrugged one shoulder. Caleb knew him well enough to sniff out a lie. "Things are a little more complicated."

"Complicated?"

He didn't flinch. "She's pregnant."

His brother's eyes bulged. "Hell! And it's yours?"

"So she says."

Caleb let out a long breath. "Do you believe her?"

"Do I have doubts?" He shrugged again. "Of course. But Mary-Jayne isn't like—"

"Like Nikki?" Caleb suggested, cutting him off. "Yeah, you're right. She seems like a real straight shooter. I know Audrey trusted her to run the store in her absence without hesitation. You gonna marry her?"

Daniel's back straightened. "Don't be stupid. I hardly know her."

Caleb grinned. "Well, you'll have plenty of opportunity to get to know her once you start raising a child together."

Raising a child together...

Daniel knew it wouldn't be that simple. She lived in Crystal Point. He lived in San Francisco. There was a hell of a lot of geography separating them. Which would make him what? A once-a-year father? Summer-vacation time or less? He was looking down the barrel at an impossible situation.

"We'll see what happens."

His brother's expression turned serious. "Tell me you're getting a paternity test?"

"Once the child is born," he said, and explained about the risks of doing the test during the second trimester.

Caleb nodded slowly. "And what do you plan to do until then?"

He shrugged a little. "It's not really up to me."

His brother made a disagreeable sound. "I can see that attitude lasting about two days," he said, and smiled. "Until the shock really hits you."

Caleb knew him well. The idea of doing nothing until the baby came sat like a lead weight in his gut. But what choice did he have? Mary-Jayne wasn't the kind of woman to take easily to being watched or hovered over. She was obviously fiercely independent and made it clear she didn't need him for anything.

Which should have put him it at ease.

Instead his insides churned. He was torn between wanting to believe her child was his and knowing it would be much better for them both if it wasn't true. But he had no real reason to disbelieve her. Sure, he thought she was a bit of a flake. But according to Solana she was honest and forthright and exactly as she seemed—a free, independent spirit who answered to no one but herself. Not the kind of woman to claim paternity when she wanted nothing in return.

"I thought I'd visit Gran," Daniel said, and sprang from the sofa. "Feel like joining me?"

Caleb shook his head and grinned as he stood. "I'm not on vacation like you. I have a business to run. And don't forget to go and see the folks this week."

"I won't," Daniel promised, and walked his brother down the hall.

Once Caleb left he locked up the villa, grabbed the keys on the hall stand and headed out. He walked around the grounds for a few minutes, and instead of going directly to Solana's villa made his way to the western side of the resort where the condos were smaller and home to many of the employees. He tapped on Mary-Jayne's door and ignored the interested looks from a few people in corporate shirts who passed him on the pathway that separated the apartments.

The door swung back and she stood in front of him. "Oh…hi."

She sounded breathless, and he was immediately concerned. "Are you okay?"

"Fine," she replied and took a deep breath. "I've been doing Pilates."

Daniel looked her over. Her hair was tied up in a haphazard ponytail and she wore black leggings and a hot pink racer-back tank top that clung to her curves. Her belly looked like it had popped out a little more overnight and he fought the unexpected urge to place his hand on her stomach. Her cheeks were flushed and her lips looked plump and red. There was something wholly healthy and attractive about her that warmed his blood.

"Pilates?" he echoed, and curled his fingers into his palms to stop himself from reaching out to touch her.

"It's good for the baby," she replied. "And me. So did you want something?"

"Only to see how you are feeling today."

"I'm fine," she said, her hand positioned on the door like she couldn't wait to close it. "How are you?"

"Okay," he said.

"Well, thanks for stopping by."

Daniel shifted on his feet. "I thought... I wondered if you would like to have lunch."

Her brows arched. "Lunch? With you? Where?"

He shrugged a little. "There are four restaurants at this resort...take your pick."

Her brows stayed high. "Beneath the prying eyes of wait staff and various employees? Isn't that a little risky? People might start thinking you've been consorting with the help."

Daniel's jaw clenched. She was an argumentative and provocative pain in the neck. And he wanted her anyway.

"First, I don't care what anyone thinks. And second, you are not *the help*, Mary-Jayne. Are you going to be difficult and refuse every request I make? Or accept that you need to eat and since you're a lousy cook anyway, it would—"

"I'm not a *lousy* cook," she retorted and a tiny smile

curved her mouth. "Just not a good cook. And while I appreciate your invitation, I'm hardly dressed for anything other than a cheese sandwich in front of the TV."

He looked her over again and his libido twitched. "I'll come back in half an hour. Unless you need help getting out of your clothes?"

For a second he thought she might slam the door in his face. But to his surprise she laughed softly. "I'm sure I can manage. Okay, see you in thirty minutes."

Then she did close the door and Daniel turned on his heels. And as he walked back down the path he realized he was grinning foolishly.

Lunch.
Great idea.
Not...

As she slipped into a knee-length white denim sundress, Mary-Jayne cursed herself repeatedly for being so agreeable and for finding Daniel Anderson charming and attractive and so darn sexy he could ask her to jet to the moon and she probably would.

She had to get a handle on the chemistry between them. There was no other option.

He tapped on her door exactly thirty minutes later and Mary-Jayne scowled as she moved down the short hallway. He was the punctual type. It figured. Everything about him screamed order and control.

She opened the door and faced him. "I'm ready."

"So I see," he said, and stood aside to let her pass.

Mary-Jayne closed the door and dropped the key into the tote draped over her left shoulder. "Where are we going?" she asked.

"Your choice," he replied. "Like I said."

Mary-Jayne took a deep breath. There were four restaurants at the resort: two bistros designed for families, a trendy Japanese teppanyaki bar and an exclusive à la carte restaurant named after his grandmother that Mary-Jayne had never been in because the menu was way out of her price range, even though Solana had offered to take her there several times.

She smiled sweetly. "Solana's. Think you'll be able to get a table at such short notice?"

His mouth turned up a little. "I'm sure they will be able to accommodate us."

Mary-Jayne looked up at him. "No one would dare defy you, would they?"

"Oh, I could think of someone who would."

He was smiling now and it made her smile back. *Keep your head.* The warning voice at the back of her mind told her to ignore the way her insides fluttered. She didn't want to *flutter* around him. She didn't want to have any kind of reaction. He was her baby's father—that was all. Besides, he didn't actually believe he had fathered her baby, so she should keep being madder than hell and resentful that he thought her so deceptive.

"Well, there's no point in going through life thinking you can have everything your own way, is there?" she replied, and started walking down the path.

He caught up with her in a few strides. "Or thinking you can say whatever you like."

Mary-Jayne stopped in her tracks. "Is that a nice way of saying I have a big mouth?"

"Actually," he said as he came to a halt beside her, "you have a very…lovely mouth."

There was something so flagrantly suggestive about his words that heat quickly travelled up her legs, belly and chest and then hit her directly in her cheeks. Memories banged around in her head. Memories of his touch.

His kiss. His possession. It was too easy to recall the crazy chemistry they shared and the night they'd spent together.

"I wish you wouldn't…"

Her words trailed off as she met his steely gaze. He had a hypnotic power that was uniquely his and it was something she'd never experienced before. She didn't *like* him. She didn't *want* him in her life. But Daniel had a way of invading her thoughts and plaguing her dreams.

"You wish I wouldn't…what?"

She sucked in a shallow breath and stepped sideways. "Stand so close," she said and crossed her arms.

A grin tugged at his mouth. As if he knew just how profoundly he affected her. And as if it pleased him no end.

"Not everything has to be a battle, Mary-Jayne."

And she wished he'd stop saying her name like that… kind of silky and smooth and sexy and impossible to ignore.

He was wrong. Everything did have to be a battle. It was the only way she'd remain unscathed. "Sure," she said and started walking again.

He stopped to make a phone call and was by the main entrance when he caught up with her. Without saying another word she followed him inside, across the foyer and then toward the elevator. The looks and stares from staff as they passed didn't go unnoticed, and Mary-Jayne suspected she'd quickly be the subject of whispers and conjecture. Since she'd arrived at the resort she'd kept to herself. She hadn't socialized with the staff or other store owners. She managed Audrey's store during the day and worked on her jewelry in the evenings. After Solana's birthday party she'd kept her head down and minded her own business, figuring others would do the same in regard to her. And mostly the staff did. Of course everyone knew about Audrey's disastrous affair with Caleb and speculation was rife that her friend had bailed simply to get away from the resort and him and avoid further humiliation. Only Mary-Jayne knew the truth. Sure, Audrey's mother was unwell...but it *was* exactly the excuse Audrey had needed to salvage her pride and put serious miles between herself and the man who'd hurt her so badly.

Mary-Jayne certainly didn't want to trade one scandal for another.

And she certainly didn't want anyone thinking she was sleeping with the boss!

"Everything all right?"

She glanced sideways and pulled her tote close to her belly. "Peachy."

"Worried what people might think?"

Her mouth tightened. He was too intuitive for her liking. "Couldn't care less."

She stepped into the elevator and he moved in behind her. He stared at her for a second before raising one dark brow. "Perhaps you're not as free-spirited as I thought."

She shrugged. "Maybe not."

The door opened, and Mary-Jayne was about to step out when she realized they weren't on the restaurant level. They were one floor up on the conference suites and boardroom level.

He touched her back and gently urged her forward. "Come on."

"Why are we here? I thought we were—"

"This way," he replied, and kept her moving down the short corridor.

A door opened at the end of the hall and a young man in white chef's gear greeted them. Mary-Jayne had seen him around the resort a few times. Daniel greeted him by name and they were shown directly into a private dining area. It was luxury personified. There were half a dozen tables covered in crisp white linen and the finest dinnerware and crystal. A long panel of windows overlooked the pool area and also offered an incredible view of the ocean.

A waiter emerged from another door and pulled out a seat at a table by the window.

Mary-Jayne rocked back on her heels and looked at Daniel. "Nice view."

"Shall we sit?"

His words were more request than question, and she fought the urge to turn around and leave. Instead she smiled a little and sat down. The waiter offered her some sparkling water, and she gave a grateful nod and only spoke again when the young man and the chef left the room.

She dropped her tote to her feet, stared out the window for a moment before resting her elbows on the table and turning her gaze toward the man sitting opposite. "Clearly I'm not the only one concerned about what people think."

He stilled. "What?"

She waved a hand vaguely. "Up the back elevator and into a secret room?"

"Private," he clarified. "Not secret. I thought you might prefer it. Personally I couldn't care less what people think."

She wondered if that were true. Daniel possessed a kind of confidence she suspected was born from arrogance. He was used to getting his own way. Used to telling people what to do. He called the shots...and she couldn't imagine him tolerating speculation from anyone in his employ.

"Well, they'll be *thinking* plenty once my belly really pops out."

His mouth curled at the edges. "They can think what they like. I should have realized you were pregnant when I first saw you yesterday," he said quietly. "It suits you."

She smirked a little. "Am I glowing?"

He nodded. "Yes."

It was a nice compliment, and her skin warmed. "I'll probably end up the size of a house, though," she said and laughed. "All the women in my family have looked like they've swallowed an elephant when they were pregnant."

His mouth curled at the sides, and it was incredibly sexy. "Tell me about them."

"My family?" She shrugged. "There's not much to tell. We all live in Crystal Point. My parents are both retired. My older brother, Noah, is married to Callie and they have four kids. He builds boats and she's a horse-riding instructor. Then there's my sister Evie, who's an artist and runs a bed-and-breakfast. She's married to Scott—who's actually Callie's brother. He's a firefighter and they have two kids. Then there's Grace, who is married to Noah's best friend Cameron. He's a cop, she's a finance broker and they had their first baby two months ago. And then there's little-old-knocked-up me."

He smiled at her words. "No...not much to tell at all."

Mary-Jayne laughed again. It occurred to her that despite how much he aggravated her, she smiled a lot around Daniel. "They're good people."

"I don't doubt it. I imagine you had a very happy childhood."

"Mostly," she admitted. "Of course it was fraught with the usual teenage-girl angst and rebellion, I suppose. I'm the youngest and therefore it's expected that I would be the most troublesome."

He grinned a little. "What kind of trouble?"

"Oh...crushes on inappropriate boys, late nights, the wrong company...and I got my tattoo at fourteen."

He grimaced. "Brave girl."

"Getting a tattoo? Brave or foolish, you mean, because basically I'm marked for life."

"I mean the pain thing."

"Pain?"

"They use needles…right?"

Mary-Jayne tilted her head. "Well…yes."

"I don't like needles."

She laughed loudly. "Chicken."

"You're mocking me," he said, his mouth twisting a little. "That's something of a habit of yours."

The waiter returned with their drinks and placed a menu on the table. Once the young man left, she returned her attention to Daniel.

"I imagine your ego is healthy enough to take it."

He grinned again. "You're probably right. So…" he said and pushed the glass around the table. "Is there any chance your father is going to come after me with a shotgun?"

She laughed loudly. "Not one. My brother, Noah, on the other hand, is very protective of his sisters." She took a long breath. "Seriously…my family let me live my own life. I'm fully prepared to raise this baby alone, Daniel. Be involved or don't. It's that simple."

His brows rose fractionally. "With me in San Francisco and you in Crystal Point? That's not simple. That's about as complicated as it gets, Mary-Jayne. Because I'm not about to avoid my legal and moral responsibility…no matter how much it seems you would like me to."

She frowned and touched her belly. "If I wanted that I would never have told you I was pregnant. Frankly, I just don't want you to get hung up on what you think you *have* to do. Sure, I'd like my baby to have a father who's involved in his or her life, but I don't want this to turn into some kind of parenting battleground with you on one side and me on the other and our child stuck in the middle."

"Nice speech. Is it meant to put me in my place?"

She shrugged. "Take it how you want. It's all rather

moot, anyhow…isn't it? Since you don't actually believe this baby is yours."

His eyes darkened and she was quickly drawn into them. Something passed between them, a kind of relentless energy that warmed her blood.

"It's not that…it's…"

"It's what?" Mary-Jayne asked, and met his gaze and asked the question hovering on her lips. "Is it because of your wife?"

Chapter Five

Daniel stilled. It was the first time the subject had been mentioned since Mary-Jayne had told him she was pregnant. Had he spared Simone more than a fleeting thought in the past twelve hours? The past twenty-four? He'd become so consumed by Mary-Jayne and the idea she was carrying his baby that he could barely think of anything else.

"I gather my grandmother told you what happened?"

She shrugged lightly. "Solana told me she was killed in a car wreck a few years ago."

"Four years," he corrected. "Four years, four months and three weeks."

Her eyes shone. "She was pregnant, wasn't she?"

He nodded slowly as his throat tightened. "Yes. Five months."

"I'm so sorry." Her hand moved across the table and connected with his for a moment before she quickly pulled it back. "It must have been devastating."

"It was the single worst day of my life."

She gathered her hands together in her lap and opened her mouth to speak when the waiter returned. Daniel watched as she studied the menu for a few seconds and then ordered one of the three vegetarian options he'd insisted be included. When she was done he ordered the swordfish, and when the waiter left he grabbed his glass and took a drink.

He put the glass down and spoke. "If you want to ask me about it, go ahead."

Her eyes widened. "You don't mind?"

He shrugged one shoulder.

"How did it happen?"

Daniel closed his eyes for a second as memories banged around in his head. He'd gone over that day countless times in his mind and the pain never lessened. "Simone was driving home from a doctor's appointment and stopped off at the mall to get a birthday gift. She pulled out of the parking lot and into the flow of traffic and a vehicle coming in the opposite direction slammed into her car. The brake line had snapped on the other car and the inexperienced driver panicked, hit the accelerator and crossed over the road."

"Was she killed instantly?"

He shook his head, almost admiring Mary-Jayne's blunt questioning. There was no false pity in her expression. Only curiosity and genuine concern.

"She died in hospital. The doctors tried to save her but her injuries were too severe."

"And the baby?"

"Our daughter died within minutes of Simone passing away."

"That's so sad. Did you have a name picked out for her?"

Daniel pushed down the heat clawing up his throat.

"We'd planned on naming her Lana, after my grand-mother."

She was quiet for a moment, her gaze lowered, clearly absorbing what he'd said. When she looked up her eyes were bright, almost glistening. He watched as she bit down on her bottom lip as moisture quickly filled her eyes. He'd observed many emotions cross her face in the time they'd known one another—anger, dislike, humor, passion—but this was something else. Sadness. Acute and heartfelt. He didn't like how it made him feel. Dealing with the combative, argumentative Mary-Jayne was easy compared to seeing her in tears.

"I'm sorry," she said, and grabbed the napkin to dab at her eyes. "I didn't mean to…" Her words trailed and she swallowed hard. "It's the baby hormones. They get me at the most unexpected times. Anyway," she said, her voice a little stronger, "thank you for telling me."

"It's not a secret. I'm sure my grandmother or Caleb would have told you the same thing had you asked them. It was an accident…and like all accidents, it was simply a series of events that merged into one terrible outcome."

She looked at him with silent intensity. "You mean, if she'd lingered at the mall a little longer, or if she had taken another exit from the parking lot, or the other driver had gotten out of bed ten minutes later that morning things would have turned out differently?"

"Exactly."

"You said she was buying a birthday gift. Who was it for?"

Daniel hesitated for a moment. "My grandmother."

It took a moment, but her eyes widened as realization dawned. "So…that night…the night of Solana's birthday party…it was the…the…"

"The anniversary of their deaths? Yes, it was."

The waiter returned with their meals before she had a chance to respond, and Daniel watched with keen interest as she took a long breath and stared into her plate. Once the waiter left them she looked up.

"Is that why you…why you…"

"Why I what?" he asked.

"The party, you know…and how we…" Her words trailed and she shrugged lightly.

"We had sex, you mean?"

Sex. He wasn't going to call it anything else. He wasn't going to suggest they'd made love because it would have been a lie. He used to make love to his wife. There was love and heart and passion between them. They'd been friends since college and started dating when Simone had finished law school. What he felt for Mary-Jayne wasn't grounded in that kind of friendship or any measure of deep emotion. It was base and instinctual and fuelled by attraction and sexual desire. And he intended for it to stay that way. She might be under his skin, but he wasn't about to let her get into his heart.

"I thought there might be a connection," she said and arched one brow. "Like you were wanting…to forget about…"

"I could never forget my wife," he said quietly.

She flinched a little. "I didn't mean that. I was thinking perhaps you needed a distraction that night and that's why you were interested in me."

"I was *interested* in you from the moment I saw you in the store window."

He knew she wouldn't be surprised by his admission. There had been heat between them from that first glance. Daniel wasn't conceited, but he knew the attraction he felt for Mary-Jayne was very much reciprocated.

"Oh…okay."

"The fact it was my grandmother's birthday was a co-incidence," he said, stretching the truth to avoid her questions or her censure. He wasn't about to admit that the hollow feeling that had haunted him since Simone's death had been amplified that night. Or that for a few incredible hours he'd found solace in the arms of a woman he barely knew. "So have you been well other than the nausea?" he asked, shifting the subject.

"Mostly," she replied. "Both my sisters suffered from gestational diabetes when they were pregnant, so my doctor is keeping watch on my sugar levels. But I feel fine at the moment."

Concern tightened his chest. "Does that mean this pregnancy holds risks for you? Is there something we should talk to your doctor about? Perhaps a second opinion is needed to ensure you get the best possible care. I can arrange an appointment with a specialist if—"

"I'm fine," she said sharply, interrupting him as she picked up the cutlery. "The nausea and appetite issues are a normal part of being pregnant. And I like my current doctor just fine, thank you. Stop interfering."

He bit back a grin at her impatience. "Don't mistake concern for control, Mary-Jayne."

She flashed him an annoyed look. "I don't."

"Oh, I think you do. I think you're so desperate to stay in control here that anything I say will be like waving a red flag at a bull."

She looked as if she wanted to jab him in the forehead with her fork. "You really do love to hear the sound of your own voice."

He laughed. "Hit a nerve, did I?"

"By implying that I value my independence?" she shot back. "Not a nerve…a fact. I'm not about to be lorded over like some spineless minion."

"That's a favorite insult of yours," he said and watched her. "Despite what you've conjured in your colorful imagination, I don't live in a house filled with servants. I cook my own meals, launder my own clothes and even tie my own shoes."

Her green eyes flashed. "Doesn't stop you from being a condescending horse's ass, does it?"

He laughed again. They had a way of pushing each other's buttons, and watching her fiery expression quickly stirred his blood and libido. "We have five months to get through until the baby comes, and I'd prefer it if we could manage that time without constantly goading one another, wouldn't you?"

She shrugged as if she couldn't have cared less. But Daniel wasn't fooled. She was as wound up as he was. "Since you'll be in San Francisco and I'll be in Crystal Point, what difference does it make?"

An ocean. Thousands of miles. A different life. There would be so many things between them. Between him and the child she carried. The child she said was his. Most of the shock had worn off overnight. Sure, he wanted a paternity test, but there were months ahead where he either had to accept the child was his, or not. And, despite everything between them, he realized that he believed Mary-Jayne. His grandmother knew her, trusted her... and although some old cynical instincts banged around in his head, Daniel realized he trusted her, too.

"You could come to San Francisco."

She looked up and made a scoffing sound. "Yeah... right."

Maybe not. "What about here?"

Her gaze sharpened. "Here? At the resort?"

"Yes."

"I can't do that, either," she said, and put down her fork.

"Why not?" he shot back. "Your jewelry business is mostly done online, so you could do that anywhere...San Francisco or here."

"This isn't my home, that's why not. I live in Crystal Point... I've lived there all my life. It's where I was born and it's where my baby will be born."

"Our baby."

Her jaw dropped slightly. "You believe me?"

He took a breath and nodded. "I believe you."

She looked wary. "Why the sudden change of heart?"

"Because *not* believing you essentially means I forfeit any rights to be part of this experience."

Mary-Jayne stilled. Rights? What did he mean by that? He wanted rights? He believed her? It should have put her at ease. Instead her entire body was suddenly on red alert. What had she expected? That once she told him about her pregnancy then he would quietly go away and leave her to raise her child alone?

Naive idiot.

The urge to get up and leave suddenly overwhelmed her, and it took all her strength to remain in her seat. She slowly met his unwavering gaze. "I'll be leaving in less than two weeks," she said. "As soon as Audrey returns I'm going home. My home," she reiterated. "Where I belong."

"Then I'll go with you," he said, so casually that her blood simmered. "We need to tell your folks, anyhow."

"I'll tell *my* family when *I* choose," she said, and pushed back her chair a fraction. "Stop bossing me about."

"Stop acting like a child."

It was the kind of verbal gridlock she expected when she was near him. They didn't like one another. They never would. They had sexual chemistry and nothing more. Fatigue and a sudden surge of queasiness shortened her patience and she pushed the seat back.

"Thanks for lunch," she said, and stood. "I'll see my own way out."

"My case in point," he said as he got up. "Run when you don't like what you hear. That's a child's way out, Mary-Jayne."

Her rage sought release. "Go to hell."

His mouth quirked fractionally. "I'll see you Tuesday morning, at nine, for the ultrasound appointment."

"I'd rather—"

"At nine," he insisted, cutting her off.

She didn't respond. Instead she grabbed her tote, thrust back her shoulders and left the room with a pounding heart, more determined than ever to keep him at arm's length.

Back in her condo she calmed down a little, took a shower and called Audrey. Her friend didn't answer her phone so she left a brief message. She spent the remainder of the day staring at her phone, hoping Audrey would call and watching an old movie on the television. By the time she dropped into bed her head was thumping and her rage was festering.

How dare he call her childish? He was an arrogant, pompous jerk! The sooner she was away from him, the better.

On Monday Mary-Jayne lay low. She opened the store and kept away from the front window as much as possible, in case *he* walked by. Or watched her. Or stalked her. But thankfully he didn't show up at the store and didn't call. And since Caleb didn't do his usual midmorning drop in either, Mary-Jayne knew Daniel had told his brother to steer clear.

Puppet master...

Controlling everything and everyone around him.

It made her mad, and got her blood boiling.

On Tuesday morning she set her alarm an hour early, showered and forced herself to eat breakfast. She dressed in a knee-length button-up blue floral dress and tied her hair up in a ponytail. Then she waited on the sofa for him to arrive, hands clasped together. He tapped on the door at nine o'clock with his usual annoying promptness.

He looked so good in jeans and a collared black T-shirt she could barely croak out a greeting when her level gaze met the broad expanse of his chest. She stupidly wished she were taller, more slender, more elegant...and able to meet his eyes without having to look up.

"Good morning."

Mary-Jayne forced out a smile. "Are you always on time for everything?"

"Always."

"It's an annoying trait of yours."

He grinned and motioned for her to pass. Once he pulled the door shut he placed a hand into the small of her back and ushered her forward. "Well, I guess it's one of those things you'll have to get used to."

Not when there's an ocean between us I won't...

By the time they were in his car she was so worked up her teeth chattered. He asked for the address and she replied quietly, staying silent as he punched the information into his GPS. Once they were on their way she dropped her tote to her feet and stared out the side window. But his nearness still rattled her. He was so close and had a kind of hypnotic power she'd never experienced before. Any man she'd ever known paled beside him. Any attraction she'd had in the past seemed lukewarm compared to the heat that simmered between them. The arguments didn't mask anything. It only amplified the undercurrent of desire and made her remember the passion and pleasure they'd shared that night four months ago.

She turned her head to glance at his profile. "Have you ever done that before?"

"Done what?"

"Sleep with someone you hardly know."

His mouth curved, but he looked straight ahead. "I don't recall either of us getting a whole lot of sleep that night."

Her cheeks heated. "You know what I mean." She swallowed hard. "I… It's just that I… Despite how I *seem*… I'm not like that…usually."

"Usually?"

She let out a heavy breath. "I don't sleep around…okay. I might come across as free-spirited and all that…but when it comes to sex I'm not easy. I've had three serious relationships including my high school boyfriend and I've never had a one-night stand before."

"Are you asking how many relationships I've had? Or one-night stands?" He glanced at her for a moment. "Does it really matter?"

His reticence irritated her and she frowned. "Is the subject off-limits for some reason?"

His jaw tightened. "My wife died over four years ago. Have I remained celibate since then? No. Have I had a committed relationship since then? No. Is that enough of an answer, Mary-Jayne?"

She got the message. She was one in a long line of meaningless one-night stands.

Just as well she didn't like him in the least, or she might have been offended by his admission. "I don't have any kind of ulterior motive for asking," she said and stared directly ahead. "I was curious, that's all."

"Well, if your curiosity has you imagining I have a

different woman in my bed every night, you'll be disappointed."

She didn't want to think about any woman in his bed, different or otherwise. "I'd have to care to feel disappointment, wouldn't I?"

"I guess you would," he said quietly. "But in case you've been having sleepless nights over it—my bed has been empty since you left it so quickly in the small hours of the morning all those months ago."

It was a dig. She'd snuck out of his villa, all right, and he clearly didn't appreciate her efforts to avoid any uncomfortable morning-after postmortems. Obviously he'd been stung by her disappearing act. And it took her a moment to realize what he'd said about his empty bed.

"No one since? Have you already nailed every woman in San Francisco? Is that the problem?"

He laughed humorlessly. "You're the problem."

"Me?" She almost squeaked the word out. "I can't imagine why."

"One night didn't really do us justice, did it? Not with that kind of instant attraction."

She knew what he meant. The store window. The resort foyer. The beach. Solana's party. Every time they'd met the heat had ramped up a notch. Until it had become so explosive the outcome was unavoidable.

"So you want...you still want..."

He chuckled. "You know, you really are a fascinating contradiction. For such a *free-spirited* woman, you can be equally shy and self-conscious."

"Because I think sex should mean something? Because I think one-night stands are empty and pointless and of little importance?"

His profile was unmoving. "Since our night together

resulted in this pregnancy, I'd say it's about as important as it gets, wouldn't you?"

She frowned. "You're twisting my words. I meant the sex wasn't important...not the baby."

There was insult in her words, and she was surprised that he stayed silent.

Silent and seething.

He was mad. Perhaps his ego wasn't as rock solid as she thought?

"That's not a complaint, by the way," she said, and pushed the tote around with her feet. "The sex was very... nice."

"It wasn't *nice*, Mary-Jayne. It was hot and incredibly erotic and about as good as it gets."

He was right. They both knew it.

"That, too," she admitted. "And the reason I left," she said, and figured she may as well tell him the truth, "is I didn't want any morning-after awkwardness. I thought it would be easier to bail and forget the whole thing. I mean, it was never going to be any more than one night. I think we both knew that."

"If I believed that I wouldn't have repeatedly asked you out."

It was true. He *had* pursued her. And she'd refused him every time. Because they were too different. As clichéd as oil and water. He wanted her in his bed and he got what he wanted. Only a fool would imagine he was looking for anything more.

"To get me into bed again, right? Which means we would have been back to square one. The point I'm making is men and women generally think about sex differently. I'm not saying I'm after a picket fence quite yet, but I'm not foolish enough to waste time on something or someone where it wouldn't be on the table ever."

"That's quite a judgment."

"Can you deny it?" she asked. "Let's face it, Daniel, you and I are polar opposites in every way. Sure, we have chemistry, but that's all. Most of the time we barely seem to tolerate one another. That's not a recipe for romance. It's a recipe for disaster."

She turned back to look out the side window with a heavy sigh, and they didn't say another word to one another until they'd reached Cairns. With a population of over one hundred thousand, the bustling regional city was a popular tourist spot and served as a starting point for people wanting to visit the Great Barrier Reef.

Within minutes they were pulling into the car park in front of the medical center. She got out of the Jeep, grabbed her tote and waited for him to come around to the passenger side.

"If you like, we can look around town when we're done," he suggested and locked the vehicle. "Maybe have lunch."

"The way you keep trying to feed me, anyone would think I need fattening up."

His brows narrowed. "Well, I have noticed you don't eat enough."

Mary-Jayne put her hands on her thickening waist. "I eat plenty. Have you seen my ever-expanding middle? I told you how the women in my family look when they're pregnant."

"You hardly touched your food the other day."

Mary-Jayne looked up at him. "I was too mad to eat."

"Too hot headed, you mean."

"You were being a bossy, arrogant jerk. It annoyed me."

"Everything I do appears to annoy you," he said and ushered her toward the steps that led into the building. "Perhaps you should consider why that is."

"I know why," she said, and moved up the steps. "Because you're a bossy, arrogant jerk."

He laughed softly and grasped her hand, stopping her before they reached the door. Mary-Jayne looked up and met his gaze. His gray eyes were dark and intense, and for a second she couldn't do anything but stare at him. The pulse in his cheek throbbed and she fought the urge to touch the spot.

He threaded their fingers and drew her closer. "How about you let me off the hook for a little while, hmm?"

Don't do it...

"I can't..."

"Sure you can," he said, and rubbed his thumb inside her palm. "I'm not your enemy, Mary-Jayne...except perhaps in your lively imagination."

"Daniel..."

"Come on," he said, and gently led her inside. "Let's go and meet this baby."

It took about twenty minutes to find the correct office, see reception and be shown to a small room when she was instructed to lie on the bed and wait for the doctor. A nurse appeared and wheeled the imaging machine close to the bed and told them the doctor would be in soon.

"Are you okay?" he asked from the chair he sat on from across the room.

Mary-Jayne lay back on the table and wiggled. "Fine. Peachy. Never better."

"You look nervous."

She shrugged. "Well, I've never done this before, so of course I'm a little nervous."

As she said the words it occurred to her that Daniel probably *had* done this before. With Simone. With the wife he'd loved and the baby they'd lost. It must have been hard for him to come into the room with her, a woman he hardly knew, and potentially have the same experience he'd shared with his wife.

Shame hit her square between the shoulders.

All morning she'd been thinking of herself and hadn't spared a thought for his feelings. *What's happened to me? When did I become so self-absorbed?*

"I'm sorry."

He looked at her. "For what?"

"For not considering how difficult it must be for you to do this."

His gaze didn't waver. "It's not difficult. Just…different. Simone and I had planned everything, from conception to her due date. She'd had endometriosis for several years and had trouble getting pregnant. Eventually we used IVF and she got pregnant after three attempts. It was all rather clinical and organized and more about the treatments and processes rather than the baby…at least in the beginning. So, yes, this is different."

There was heat in her throat. "Okay," she said, and smiled a little. "You're off the hook."

The doctor came into the room then and Daniel got to his feet. Mary-Jayne lay back and tried to relax. He moved beside her and touched her shoulder.

"So," Doctor Stewart said once she'd introduced herself and perched on a stool at the side of the bed. "Would you like to know your baby's sex?"

Mary-Jayne looked at Daniel.

He shrugged lightly. "It's up to you."

She swallowed hard. "I think… Yes…I'd like to know."

She glanced at him again and thought he looked relieved.

The doctor got her to unbutton her dress, and Mary-Jayne tried not to be self-conscious of Daniel's presence in the chair at her side as her belly was bared. A cool gel was placed on her stomach and she shivered a little. Daniel took hold of her hand and squeezed gently.

Once the ultrasound started she was riveted to the image on the small screen. It didn't look like anything at first, until the doctor pointed out an arm and the baby's head. Emotion welled inside her and she bit back a sob.

Hi there, peanut... I'm your mother...and I love you more than I thought possible.

"And there's your baby," the doctor said, and rolled the device lower. "You have a perfectly lovely boy."

She looked at Daniel and noticed he stared directly at the screen, clearly absorbed by what they saw. He'd never looked more attractive to her, and in that moment an unexpected surge of longing rushed through her entire body.

Longing and desire and something else...something she couldn't quite fathom.

Something she didn't want to think about.

"Oh..."

The doctor's voice quickly cut through her thoughts.

"What is it?"

Daniel's voice now. Deep and smooth and quicker than usual. It gave her comfort. If something was wrong, he was there, holding her hand, giving her strength. He glanced at her and squeezed her fingers.

Doctor Stewart looked at them both. "Well...I see."

"What?" he asked again, firmer this time. "Is something wrong?" It was the question she was too afraid to ask.

"Nothing's wrong," the doctor said, and smiled broadly. "It's just...there are two of them."

Mary-Jayne stared at the screen. "What do you mean?"

The doctor smiled. "Congratulations to you both... you're having twin boys."

Chapter Six

Someone could have told him that he was going to live on the moon for the next fifty years and he wouldn't have been more shocked.

Twin boys...

"You're sure?" he asked the doctor, and noticed how Mary-Jayne hadn't moved. He squeezed her hand reassuringly. "And they're fine?"

The doctor nodded. "Fine. Big, strong and healthy. Would you like to listen to their heartbeats?"

Daniel didn't recall saying yes. But within seconds he had small earphones on and heard the incredible sound of his sons' hearts. Emotion rose up and hit him directly in the solar plexus, polarizing him for a moment. He swallowed hard, fighting the heat in his eyes and throat. Nothing he ever heard again would match the sound of the two tiny heartbeats pounding almost in unison. Longing, absolute and raw, filled his chest with such force he grabbed the side of the chair for support.

The doctor said something about having a picture done for them, but he barely heard. He took off the earphones and gently placed them over Mary-Jayne's head. Watching her expression shift from shock to wonderment was incredible. Her face radiated with a joy so acute it was blinding in its intensity. She'd never looked more beautiful.

The doctor stood. "I'll arrange for a picture and come back in a little while," she said, and quickly left the room.

Daniel tightened his grip on Mary-Jayne's hand. "Are you okay?"

She dropped the earphones onto the bed. "Um…I think so."

"Not what you were expecting, huh?"

She sighed. "Not exactly. But…" Her words trailed off for a moment. "I'm happy." She glanced at the now-blank screen. "I can't quite believe it."

"Are there many twins in your family?" he asked, and rubbed her fingertips. She shrugged. "Not really. I know there are in yours, though."

He nodded and grinned. "Yes. My brothers are twins. My grandfather was a twin, and I have two sets of cousins who are twins. It's like an epidemic in my family."

"This is all your doing, then?" she said and smiled.

"I don't think there's actually a genetic link on the father's side, but I'll happily take the credit if you want," he said softly. "Are you okay with this?"

"I'm happy, like I said. And a little scared. I wasn't expecting two." She looked down at her naked stomach. "I wonder if the nurse will come back to get this goo off my belly."

Daniel released her hand and got up. He found a box of tissues on the counter and came back to her side. "This should do it," he said as he sat down and began wiping the gel off her skin.

It was the most intimate thing they'd done in months, and even though he acted as perfunctory as he could, it didn't stop a surge of desire from climbing up his spine. She lay still, perfectly composed. Until he met her gaze and saw that she was watching him with scorching intensity. When he was done her hand came up and she grabbed his fingertips and then gently laid his palm against her belly. She placed her hand on top of his, connecting them in a way that was mesmerizing. Feeling her, feeling their babies, Daniel had no answer for the sensation banging around in his head.

He'd never wanted to feel this again. Not after Simone.

But it was inevitable. They were his children. His sons. They were part of him. How could he not get drawn into feeling such acute and blinding love for them? He couldn't. And he wanted them. He wanted to be part of their lives. Full-time. A real parent.

A real father.

He looked at Mary-Jayne. Her eyes were bright. Luminous. She chewed on her bottom lip and his gaze immediately went to her mouth. He touched her forehead with his other hand and felt the connection down deep. Soul-deep.

In that moment he could nothing else but kiss her.

And her lips, as new as they were familiar, softened beneath his instantly. Daniel's pulse quickened as the kiss quickly deepened. Her breath was warm, her tongue accepting when he sought it with his own. She sighed deep in her throat, and a powerful surge of desire wound through his blood. He touched her hair, twirling the glorious strands between his fingertips. Her hand came up to his chest and he felt the connection through to his bones. And he kissed her again. And again. With each kiss his need for her grew. As did the knowledge he had one option. One way to make things right.

"Mary-Jayne," he said against her lips, trailing his mouth down her cheek to the sensitive spot by her earlobe. A spot he knew made her quiver. "We should get married."

She stilled instantly. Her mouth drew in a tight line and she pushed his hand off her belly. "What?"

Daniel pulled back and stared into her face. "Married," he said again. "We should get married."

She put a hand on his shoulder and gave him a shove. "Don't be ridiculous."

He straightened and got to his feet. "It's the only solution."

"To what?" she said, and pulled her dress closed over her stomach as she swung her legs off the bed. "Since there's no problem, we don't need a solution." She swiftly buttoned up her dress.

He crossed his arms. "There *is* a problem. We're having two children together and we live on opposite sides of the world."

"I said you can see the baby...I mean, babies, as much as you want. But I'm not interested in a loveless marriage, Daniel. Not with you or anyone else."

The doctor returned before he had an opportunity to say anything more. She gave them the photo of the twins and advised Mary-Jayne to make another appointment with her obstetrician in the next few weeks. Daniel listened while she briefly explained how she was returning home to Crystal Point in the next fortnight and how she would see her family doctor once she was back home.

Home...

He almost envied the way she spoke about the tiny town where she'd lived all her life. Nowhere felt like home to Daniel. Not Port Douglas. Not San Francisco.

They left a few minutes later and Mary-Jayne didn't

say a word as they made their way out of the building toward their vehicle.

"Are you hungry?" he asked as he opened the passenger door. "We could stop somewhere for—"

"I'd prefer to just go back to the resort," she said, cutting him off. "I'm a little tired."

Daniel didn't argue. He nodded and closed the door once she was inside. They were soon back on the road, and he made a quick stop to refuel and grab a couple of bottles of water. She took the water with a nod and tucked it by the seat. Fifteen minutes into their return trip he'd had enough of her unusual silence and spoke.

"Avoiding the subject isn't going to make it go away, Mary-Jayne."

"What subject?"

"My proposal."

She glanced sideways. "I thought you must have been joking."

"I'm perfectly serious. Once you calm down you'll realize it's the only thing we can do."

She huffed. "I'm perfectly calm. And marrying you is the *last* thing I want to do."

"Why not?" he asked, ignoring how much disdain she had in her voice.

"Because I'm not in the market for someone like you."

"Like me?" He smiled at her relentless insults. "Straight, healthy and financially secure?"

"Arrogant, judgmental and a pain in the—"

"Don't you think our children deserve two parents?"

"Our children *will* have two parents," she said, her knuckles white where she clasped her hands together. "Two parents who live in different countries. Two parents who have too much good sense to marry because it's expected they should." She turned her head. "Be honest, Daniel. You don't want to marry me, you just think you *have* to. But you don't. You're off the hook here. So please, don't mention it again."

He pushed down his irritation. She wound him up like no one else ever had. "I take it you're not opposed to marriage entirely…just marriage to me?"

"I'm opposed to marrying someone I don't love," she said bluntly. "And someone who doesn't love me. The thing is, I believe in love…and I want it. I want to be with someone who wants *me* above all others. Who wants only me and sees only me and who carries only me close to his heart."

It was foolish and romantic nonsense. "How can that matter when there are children involved?"

"Because it does," she insisted. "You've had some attack of conscience since you saw them on that screen and think marriage will somehow uncomplicate this…but it won't. We're too different to be tied to one another for life. And I'm not criticizing your motives, I'm simply trying to do what's best for everyone involved…including you."

Daniel wasn't convinced. His father and stepmother had married because Bernie was pregnant, and their marriage had turned out fine. They'd scraped a family together despite their differences. And if he was going to have any chance of being a hands-on father to his sons, Daniel knew he had to do the same.

But he knew Mary-Jayne well enough to recognize she wasn't prepared to discuss it any further. At least for now.

"We'll talk about it later."

"No, we won't," she reaffirmed. "And what was with that kiss?"

"It was a kiss. People kiss, Mary-Jayne."

She pointed to him and then herself. "Well, not *these* people. Don't do it again."

Had he lost his mind?

Marriage? As if she'd ever agree to that? Couldn't he see it was madness? He'd married for love once...how could he be prepared to settle for anything less? He could still be a father to their children. Sure, it would be challenging, considering the miles between them. But they could make it work. Plenty of people did the same. He was simply being bullheaded about it. Wanting his own way. Trying to control her.

Well, she wasn't about to be maneuvered into a loveless marriage.

She didn't care how much chemistry they had.

And he better not try to kiss her again, either!

"I'd like to stop and see my parents and tell them the news, if that's okay with you?"

Mary-Jayne turned her head. "Sure. Whatever."

It was a small detour, but she didn't mind. She liked Miles and figured they had to start telling people about the babies at some point. It took about half an hour to reach their small hobby farm, and Mary-Jayne sat up straight as he turned off into a narrow driveway and drove half a mile down the bumpy road until they reached the house. She saw the lovely timber home with wide verandas and noticed a small structure built in replica.

"My dad's studio," Daniel explained.

She turned her head. He watched her with such intensity for a moment her breath stuck in her throat. There was something riveting about his gaze, and she turned hot all over. She foolishly thought about the kiss again. It had been sweet and hot and had stirred her libido.

People kiss...

His words fluttered around in her head. Of course she knew it had been a spur-of-the-moment thing—they were looking at their babies for the first time, he'd helped remove the gel from her belly... No wonder she'd kissed him back so eagerly. She was only human. But he had an agenda. He'd decided what he wanted and would use whatever method he could to achieve that goal—which included seducing her!

She stared at him. "Please, Daniel...don't..."

"Don't what?" A smile creased the corners of his mouth. "What have I done now?"

"You know what," she said, pretty sure she sounded like a petulant child but not caring. "You kissed me."

"You kissed me back."

Color spotted her cheeks. "Well, I'm not going to be swept up in a whole lot of sex stuff...if that's what you're thinking."

He laughed as though he thought her hilarious. "I guess time will tell."

She seethed. "Just because you got me into bed once doesn't mean you will again. That night was out of character for me. I don't even *like* you."

Daniel sat back and turned the engine off. "Is this your usual mode of defense, Mary-Jayne? Attack first?"

She made a scoffing sound. "That's rich, coming from you. You're the corporate shark, not me."

"What is it exactly that you think I do for a living—steamroll over whoever gets in my way? I hate to disappoint you, but I'm not that mercenary. I'm the CEO of a large business that employs several thousand people around the globe. I'm not sure what it is you find so disagreeable about that or me."

"Everything," she replied. "Your arrogance for one...

like right now when you think I'm loopy because I dare to admit that I don't like you."

"I think you're scared," he said quietly. "Not loopy. And I think your emotions are heightened because you're pregnant."

Logically, she knew he was right. But he wound her up in a way that fueled every rebellious streak she possessed. And she was fairly certain he knew it.

"It's not baby brain," she shot back. "This is *me*. Emotional and loopy."

He made an exasperated sound. "Can we put a hold on this conversation? My dad is on his way over."

Sure enough, Miles Anderson was walking toward them from his studio, one strap of his shabby overalls flapping in the breeze. At sixty, he was still handsome and fit, and Mary-Jayne got a snapshot of what Daniel would be like in thirty years. The notion made her insides flutter. *Stupid*. She had to concentrate on now, not some time in the unknown future.

Daniel got out of the vehicle and Mary-Jayne remained where she was for the moment, watching as the two men greeted one another and shook hands. No embrace. No obvious display of affection. It saddened her a little. Would Daniel be like that with his own sons? He spoke to his father for a moment and then turned back toward the Jeep. Mary-Jayne was half out by the time he met her at the door. Miles wasn't far behind, and he watched as his son helped her out of the car.

"Lovely to see you again M.J.," Miles said cheerfully.

"Mary-Jayne," Daniel corrected, as though his father had committed the crime of the century.

She grabbed her tote and looked up at him. "No one really calls me that," she said quietly as he closed the door. "Except my folks...and you."

His mouth twitched. "It's your name."

"It's an old-fashioned mouthful."

"I think it's very pretty," Miles said, and took her arm. "Let's get up to the house. Bernie will be delighted you're here."

She could feel Daniel behind her as they walked toward the house. Mary-Jayne made a comment about how lovely the gardens were and Miles began chatting about the vegetable patch, the chickens and the new milking goat he'd recently bought who kept getting into the yard and eating the zucchini flowers.

Once they reached the veranda Miles spoke again. "My wife has a client in half an hour, but we have time for coffee and some of her pecan cookies."

Mary-Jayne noticed a door to the left of the main door and the shingle that hung to one side—Homeopath, Masseuse and Acupuncturist. Daniel's stepmother came through the open doorway, wearing a blue-and-gold tunic over white trousers, her blond hair flowing. She rushed toward him with a happy squeal and gave him a long hug.

"I'm so glad to see you," she said, all breathless energy, as they pulled apart. "Your brother told us you were back. Four months in between visits is too long."

He is loved.

It was all Mary-Jayne could think of. And then she realized how lucky her babies would be to have two such lovely people as grandparents. Her hand moved instinctively to her belly, and she noticed how Bernie's gaze immediately shifted toward the movement. She looked as though she was about to say something when Daniel stepped back and introduced them.

"It's lovely to meet you," Bernie said, smiling broadly. "Solana has told me all about you, of course. You've made quite an impression on my mother-in-law, and she's the best judge of character I know."

Mary-Jayne returned the smile. "Thank you."

Bernie tapped her husband's shoulder. "Why don't you take Daniel to the studio and show him the piece you're working on for the Phuket renovation, and Mary-Jayne and I will make coffee," she suggested, and then looked back toward Mary-Jayne. "My talented husband is sculpting an incredible bronze for the resort's foyer," she explained animatedly. "It's a dolphin pod diving through a wave." She sighed and smiled. "Just breathtaking."

Mary-Jayne grinned at the other woman's enthusiasm. She liked her immensely. "How lovely," she said, and noticed Miles looked faintly embarrassed by the praise. Daniel stood beside her, unmoving. She tapped his shoulder lightly, trying not to think about how her fingertips tingled at the connection. "You go, I'll be fine."

"Of course she will be," Bernie said, and linked their arms.

They headed inside and into the huge red cedar kitchen in the center of the house. Mary-Jayne noticed the dream catchers in nearly every window and smiled. A large pebbled water feature took up almost an entire wall, and the sound of the water slipping gently over the rocks created a charming ambience and feeling throughout the house.

"You have a lovely home," she said and perched onto a stool behind the wide kitchen counter.

"Thank you. We've been here for nearly ten years. We wanted somewhere where Miles could work without disturbing the neighbors," she said and grinned as she fiddled with the coffee machine. "Sometimes the soldering and battering goes on for hours. But we love it here and we wanted a place where our boys could call home. You know, for when they get married and have families of their own."

The innuendo wasn't missed and she dropped her gaze, took a breath and then met the other woman's inquisitive look head-on. "Yes, I'm pregnant. And yes, Daniel is the father. And we just learned we're having twin boys."

Bernie's beaming smile was infectious, and she came around the counter and hugged her close for a few seconds. "I'm so delighted. He deserves some happiness in his life after what he's been through."

Mary-Jayne was pretty sure Daniel wouldn't consider her a tonic for unhappiness.

"He loved his wife a lot, didn't he?" she asked quietly when the other woman moved back around the bench.

Bernie shrugged a little. "Simone? Well, she was easy to love. She was a nice woman, very kind and good-hearted. She was a lawyer, you know, very successful one, too, from all accounts."

As the other woman made coffee for the men and tea for them, Mary-Jayne fiddled with the silver ring on her right hand. She wasn't sure how she felt knowing Daniel had loved his wife so much. Not jealous—that would be plain stupid. Because it would mean she had feelings invested in him. Which she didn't. But displaced. As though she didn't quite belong. She wasn't someone whom Daniel would *choose* to bring home to meet his parents. Or choose to marry. She was there because she was carrying his babies. If she hadn't gotten pregnant that night they spent together then they probably would never have seen one another again.

"I'm sure she was lovely," she said and smiled.

"Daniel doesn't talk much about her," Bernie remarked, and grabbed four mugs. "He's always been a little closed off from his feelings. When Simone and their unborn baby died he kind of turned inward. The only person he really opens up to is Solana—they're very close. He never knew his real mother," she said and sighed. "I've always treated him like my own, of course. He was just a toddler when the twins were born. But I think losing his mother had a profound impact on him. And Miles grieved for a long time," she said candidly. "Even after we married and had our sons he was still mourning her death. I tried not to take it personally. I still don't on those times when he mentions her."

Mary-Jayne didn't miss the message in the other woman's words. But the situations weren't the same. She was sure Miles Anderson loved Bernadette, even if he had still grieved the wife he lost. Whereas Daniel didn't even *like* her. He might want her in his bed, but that was all it was.

"Thanks for the talk," Mary-Jayne said and smiled. "And the support."

"Anytime," Bernie said just as the men walked in through the back door.

Mary-Jayne swiveled on the stool and looked at Daniel. "How's the sculpture look?"

"Good."

Miles clapped a hand onto his son's shoulder. "Why don't you take her to the studio and show her?" he suggested, then winked at Mary-Jayne. "I should've guessed a brilliantly creative girl like you might want to critique my work. Go easy on this old man, though. My fragile artistic ego can't take too much criticism."

Mary-Jayne laughed. She genuinely liked Miles and understood his self-effacing humor. "Of course," she said and slid off the stool.

Daniel watched the interaction in silence and only moved when she took a few steps toward the door. "Coming?" she asked.

She was through the door and down the back steps quickly and didn't wait for him to catch up as she headed across the yard toward the studio. She was already inside and staring at the huge bronze sculpture when he came up behind her.

"Wow," she said as she stepped around the piece and admired the effort and imagination that had gone into its creation. "This is incredible."

Daniel came beside her. "He'll be delighted you approve."

She looked up and raised a brow. "I suppose you told him, then."

"About the babies?" He nodded. "Yes. He's delighted about that, too. Told me it was about time I settled down and raised a family."

"I hope you set him straight?"

"You mean did I tell him you've turned down my proposal? No, I thought I'd try my luck again before I admitted that."

Mary-Jayne offered a wry smile. "One marriage proposal in a day is enough, thanks very much."

"Even if I get down on my knee this time?" he asked, his eyes glittering. "Or get you a ring?"

"You're too uptight to get your kneecap dirty," she shot back, saccharine sweet. "And I want to design my own ring when I *eventually* get married."

He laughed, and she liked the sound way too much. "So, how'd Bernie take the news?"

"Very well. Tell me something, why do you call her Bernie? She's the only mother you've known, right?"

"I call her Mom sometimes," he said, looking just a little uncomfortable. "And stop cross-examining me."

"Gotta take the chance when I can. They're very nice," she said and moved around the sculpture some more. "And they love you."

"I know that," he said, and came closer again. "We just live different lives."

"But you had a happy childhood?"

He shrugged loosely. "I guess. Although there were times when I wished they'd stop moving the furniture around the house to accommodate their feng shui beliefs or eat a steak and fries instead of tofu burgers. Or have an aspirin for a headache instead of Bernie's acupuncture jabs to the temple."

Mary-Jayne stilled and looked up at him. "Is that why you don't like needles?"

"Well, I—"

She was mortified when she realized what it meant. "They stuck needles into their child?"

"They thought they were doing the right thing," he said and moved around behind her.

She turned to face him and looked up. "But that's why you don't like needles?"

"I guess," he said and shrugged again. "Seems foolish to make that kind of connection, though. It was a long time ago and it wasn't as if it was some kind of deliberate torture. Bernie's well qualified in her field and she thought she was helping. They were good parents."

"I know. And we'll be good, too," she assured him. "We've had good role models."

"Good parents who live in two different countries?" He reached out and touched a lock of her hair, twirling it between his fingertips. "I want to be their father, Mary-Jayne. All I'm asking for is a chance to do that."

Her heart tugged, and she pushed back a sudden swell of emotion "I can't. It wouldn't work," she implored. "Look, I'm not saying it's going to be easy doing this with the situation being what it is. We both know there will be challenges, especially as the children get older. But I can't and won't commit to a loveless marriage. I want what my parents have, and I want to raise my children in the town I've lived in all my life." She moved back fractionally and his hand dropped. "And I know you think that's all a load of overly romantic hogwash, but I can't change who I am and what I believe any more than you can. I've never really been in love. But I want to be."

"Yeah," he said, and shook his head. "And you want some romantic sap to carry you next to his heart… I heard all that the other day."

"But did you listen? Love isn't an illusion, Daniel. You loved your wife, right? Bernie said she was smart and beautiful and how everyone adored her. So if love was good enough for you back then, why do you think I'm so foolish for wanting the same thing?"

"Because it doesn't last."

"It does," she refuted. "Our parents are testament to that."

"So maybe sometimes it does last. But when it doesn't… When it's gone it's about as bad as it gets."

There was real pain in his voice, and she unconsciously reached out and grasped his upper arm. The muscles were tight and bunched with tension, and she met his gaze head on.

"You're still hurting," she whispered, fighting the need to comfort him.

He looked down into her face, his expression unmoving. The pulse in his cheek throbbed, and his gray eyes were as dark as polished slate. Her fingers tingled where she touched him, and when he reached up and cupped her cheek Mary-Jayne's knees wobbled.

"Most days…most days I'm just…numb."

Every compassionate and caring instinct she possessed was quickly on red alert. "It was an accident, Daniel. A terrible accident. And she wouldn't want you to feel this way, would she?"

"No," he said and traced her cheek with his thumb. "She'd want me to marry you and raise our sons together. And that's what we're going to do, Mary-Jayne. We have to get married. For the sake of our sons. All you need to do is say yes."

Chapter Seven

She didn't say yes. She didn't say anything. Instead she pulled away from him and headed back inside. They stayed for another twenty minutes, and when Bernie's client showed up they said their goodbyes and Daniel promised to return to see them in a couple of days. Being around his family made her long for her own, and Mary-Jayne stayed quiet on the trip back to the resort.

All you need to do is say yes...

As if it was so easy.

She almost admired his perseverance. Almost. He was relentless when he wanted something. No wonder he was so successful professionally. Solana had told her that he'd pretty much singlehandedly turned the chain of Sandwhisper Resorts into a flourishing enterprise around the globe. When his grandfather had been at the helm, Anderson's had only recently ventured into the new direction after spending years in copper and ore mining. Most of that was sold off now and the business focused on the resorts. While other empires had failed, Daniel had kept Anderson's afloat by using natural business acumen and innate tenacity. She remembered how he'd told her how so many people relied on the company for their livelihood and that was what made him determined to keep the organization growing.

Once they got back to the resort, he walked her to her door and lingered for a moment. "Can I see you tonight?"

Mary-Jayne shook her head. "I don't think so."

His eyes flashed. "You can't avoid me. I'm not going away, and neither is this situation."

"I'm tired, that's all. It's been a long day. And eventful," she said, and waved the envelope that held the picture of their babies.

He nodded. "All right, Mary-Jayne, I'll back off for tonight. But we have to get this sorted out."

"Yes," she said, and sighed heavily. "And we will. Just not today."

He left her reluctantly, and once he was gone she moved into the living room and slumped into the sofa. She was more confused than ever. *Daniel* confused her. Confounded her. He was relentless about the marriage thing. But she wouldn't change her mind. She couldn't. It would be a complete disaster.

She wanted love...not duty. Maybe he wasn't quite the closed-off corporate shark she'd first thought him to be; maybe there were moments when she enjoyed his company and liked the way they verbally sparred. And maybe there *was* a constant undercurrent of attraction and desire between them that made her head spin. But it still wasn't enough. And it never would be. Attraction alone wasn't enough. And those few unexpected moments where she relaxed around him were unreliable.

She hung around the condo for the remainder of the afternoon and at five o'clock was about to call Audrey again when there was a knock on her door. She groaned, loathing the thought of going another round with Daniel when all she wanted to do was talk to her friend and then curl into bed.

But it wasn't Daniel at her door. It was his grandmother.

"Can I come in?" Solana asked.

Mary-Jayne stepped back and opened the door wider. "Of course."

Once they were both settled in the living room, Solana spoke again.

"My grandson came to see me," she said and smiled. "He told me you were expecting twin boys."

Mary-Jayne wasn't surprised. It was the last thing he'd said to her when he'd walked her to her door earlier that day. He'd announced how he planned telling his grandmother about her pregnancy.

She nodded. "Yes, I am."

"And are you happy about it?"

"Very," she admitted. "I'm sorry I haven't told you earlier. Things were a little complicated and I—"

"You don't need to explain yourself. Daniel told me what happened."

She was relieved Solana understood. "Thank you. I know it must be something of a shock."

The older woman smiled. "Well, I was lining you up for Caleb...but now I think about it, you are definitely much better suited to Daniel. He needs someone who won't let him rule the roost. Caleb is way too easygoing. Whereas Daniel," Solana grinned widely, "is as wound up as a spring. You'll be good for him, I'm sure of it."

Mary-Jayne perched on the edge of the sofa. "Oh, it's not like that. We're not together or anything," she explained, coloring hotly. "I mean, we were *together*…just that once…but not now."

Solana's brows raised. "He said you've refused his marriage proposal."

"I did," she replied. "I had to. Please try to understand."

"I do," Solana said gently. "You want to fall in love and be swept off your feet. You want roses and moonlight and real romance."

"Yes," she admitted. "Exactly."

"And my grandson is too sensible and pragmatic for all that, right?"

Mary-Jayne shrugged. "We're not in love. We never would be. It would be a catastrophe."

Solana got up and moved to sit beside her on the sofa. "My son Miles married his first wife after dating her for two years. They were more in love than I'd ever seen two people in love. When she died so soon after Daniel was born Miles was heartbroken. And then along came Bernie and a few months later she was pregnant. It wasn't a love match at first…but they've made a good marriage together and raised three boys into the finest men I know."

She ignored the heavy thump behind her ribs. It was a nice story. But it's wasn't hers and Daniel's. "I know you want to see your grandson happy, but believe me, I could never be the person to do that. We don't even *like* one another."

Solana's hand came out and she briefly touched her stomach. "Oh, I'd say you liked one another well enough."

"That's not love…that's…"

"It's a place to start, that's all," Solana said. "Don't make a rash decision because you're scared of the future. Work on the present and let the future take care of itself."

It was a nice idea. But Mary-Jayne wasn't convinced.

Once the other woman left, she returned to her pacing.

She wasn't about to marry a man she didn't love. She might want him. She might even like him a little bit. Maybe more than a little bit. Maybe she liked him a lot. But it wasn't enough. It would never be enough. And she wasn't about to be railroaded into something she didn't want.

The phone rang and she snatched it up. It was Audrey.

"Thank God," she said, and quickly explained what was happening to her concerned friend.

Fourteen hours later Mary-Jayne was on a flight home.

She was gone.
Gone...
Again.

Daniel's mood shifted between concern and rage and in varying degrees.

How could she leave without a word?

Damn it, they were his children, too. His flesh. His blood.

He'd knocked on her door on Wednesday afternoon after Caleb had called and told him the store was closed again. He knocked and waited, and when she didn't respond he called her cell. It went to message and he hung up. On Thursday morning Audrey Cooper answered the door. And he knew instantly that she'd bailed. Her friend was of little help and regarded him with barely concealed contempt. The pretty redhead stood in the doorway, arms crossed, defiant and clearly willing to go into battle for her friend.

"Is she back in Crystal Point with her family?" he asked, his rage simmering, his patience frayed.

Audrey pushed back her hair, clearly unimpressed. "I'm not saying. But wherever she is, there's no point in going after her. I think it's fairly clear she doesn't want to see or hear from you."

"She said that?"

Audrey, who evidently had as much contempt for him as she did for Caleb, nodded slowly. "If you go after her she'll spook and disappear."

It sounded a little melodramatic. Mary-Jayne wouldn't do that. She wouldn't put their babies at risk. Not for anything. He knew her well enough to realize that. "That doesn't make sense."

Audrey's brows rose sharply. "I know M.J. way better than you do. She doesn't like to be hemmed in, and if you push her she'll react and run. She's got friends all over the place and they and her family would do anything for her...and that includes helping her avoid you at all costs. Just leave her alone."

Run? Jesus...she wouldn't... Would she?

Audrey grabbed the door and closed it a little. "Since you own this place, I should tell you I'm looking for someone to take over the lease on the store. If I can't find anyone in a week I'm closing up and leaving. So if you want to sue me for breach of contract, go right ahead. And tell that lousy brother of yours to stay out of my way."

Then she closed the door in his face.

Daniel was furious by the time he reached Caleb's office. His brother was sitting at his desk, punching numbers into the computer.

"Your redhead is back," he said when the door was shut.

Caleb almost jumped out of his chair. "Audrey?"

"Yeah."

"Is she still…"

"Angry?" Daniel nodded. "She hates you as much as ever and me by association, which is why she wouldn't confirm that Mary-Jayne has gone home."

His brother grabbed his jacket off the back of the chair. "I'm going to see her. Is she at the—"

Daniel pulled the jacket from his brother's hands and tossed it on the desk. "You'd better not. She's leaving the resort, closing up the store if she can't find someone to take on her lease."

Clearly agitated, Caleb grabbed the jacket again. "She can't do that. She signed a contract. We'll get the lawyers to make sure she—"

"Stop being such a hothead," Daniel said, and took the jacket, throwing it onto the sofa by the door. "And leave the lawyers out of it. She's angry and hurt and has every reason to hate you, so if she wants to leave and break the lease agreement then she can do just that...without any interference from you, understand?"

Caleb glared at him. "When did you get so sentimental?"

"When I realized that Audrey has probably already contacted Mary-Jayne and told her I'm looking for her."

His brother's temper calmed a little. "Okay, I get the point. You're concerned Mary-Jayne might do something rash."

"Actually," he said, calmer now, "I think she'll do whatever is best for the babies. Which in her eyes is going home to be around her family."

"And that's where you're going?"

He shrugged. "I have to make this right."

Caleb raised an eyebrow. "You sure you want to make a commitment to a woman you don't love? Hell, you don't even know for sure if those babies are yours."

"I do know," he said. He wound back the irritation he felt toward his brother and tapped his hand to his chest. "I feel it...in here."

And that, he figured, was all that mattered.

Mary-Jayne had been holed up in her small house for four days. Her family knew she was back, but she'd insisted she had a bad head cold and said she needed some time to recover. Her mother had tutted and pleaded to bring her some soup and parental comfort, but Mary-Jayne wasn't prepared for them quite yet. Her sisters called every day and her friend Lauren did the same. Her dog, Pricilla, and parrot, Elvis, were happy she was home and gave her all the company she needed. While she waited for Daniel to turn up. Which she knew he would.

He wasn't the kind of man to give up when he wanted something.

Mary-Jayne had no illusions… His proposal was only about their children. He didn't want to marry *her*. And she didn't want to marry him. He was single-minded in his intent… He wanted the babies. He'd take her, too, if it meant getting full-time custody of their sons.

She wondered what his next move would be. And made herself sick to the stomach thinking about the possibilities. Since she'd refused his outrageous proposal, would he try another tack? Was he thinking about sole custody? Would he fight her in court to get what he wanted? He had money and power, and that equated to influence. He could afford the finest lawyers in the country and they'd certainly be out to prove she was less capable of giving their children the best possible life. Maybe the courts would see it that way, too.

By Sunday morning she was so wound up she wanted to scream. And cry. And run.

But she wouldn't do any of those things. She needed to stay strong and focus on growing two healthy babies. She'd fight the fight she needed to when she faced it head on. Until then, her sons were all that mattered.

When Evie and Grace arrived at her door late on Sunday afternoon she was almost relieved. She hated lying to her sisters, even if it was only by omission.

One look at her and Evie squealed. "Oh, my God, you're pregnant!"

"Well, don't tell the whole neighborhood," she said, and ushered them both inside.

Grace, who was easily the most beautiful woman Mary-Jayne had ever known, was a little less animated. She'd also had her first child two months earlier. But Evie, ever the nurturer, who had a seventeen-year-old son and a toddler daughter, was still chattering as Mary-Jayne closed the door and ushered them down the hallway.

"Tell us everything," Evie insisted as the trio dropped onto the big chintz sofa. "And first the part about how you've managed to keep from spilling the beans about this."

"Forget that," Grace said and smiled. "First, tell us who the baby's father is?"

"Babies," Mary-Jayne said and waited a microsecond before her sisters realized what she meant.

There were more shrieks and laughter and a load of questions before Mary-Jayne had an opportunity to explain. It took several minutes, and when she was done each of her sisters had a hold of her hands.

"And he wants to marry you?" Grace asked.

She shrugged. "That's what he says."

Evie squeezed her fingers. "But you don't want to marry him, M.J.?"

She screwed up her face. "Definitely not."

"Is he that awful?"

She opened her mouth to respond, but quickly stopped herself. She couldn't, in good conscience, make out as if he was some kind of ogre. Once he'd settled into the idea that he was the father he'd been incredibly supportive. And she couldn't forget his caring behavior when she'd had the ultrasound.

And then there was that kiss.

Don't forget the kiss...

Of course she needed to forget the kiss. It shouldn't have happened. It had only confused her. "He's not awful," she said and sat back in the chair. "Most of the time he's quite...nice."

Grace frowned. "Most?"

"Well, he can also be an arrogant jerk," she replied. "You know, all that old money and entitlement."

"Is he tall, dark and handsome to go along with all that old money?" Evie asked and grinned.

"Oh, yeah. He's all that. And more."

"And you *still* don't want to marry him?"

"I want to marry for love," she said and sighed. "Like you both did. I don't want to settle for a man who looks at me as some kind of incubator. We might have a whole lot of chemistry now, but when that goes what's left? An empty shell disguised as a marriage? No, thanks."

"That's a fairly pessimistic view of things," Grace remarked. "And not like you at all."

"I'm tired of being the eternal optimist," she said, feeling stronger. "Being pregnant has changed my thinking. I want to build a good life for my babies—one that's honest and authentic. And if I married Daniel I would be living a lie. Despite how much I..." She stopped and let her words trail.

"Despite how much you *like* him, you mean?" Evie prompted.

She shrugged again. "Sure, I like him. But I dislike him, too, and that's where it gets complicated."

"Maybe you're making it more complicated than it needs to be," Grace suggested. "I mean, you don't really know him very well. Perhaps over time you will change your mind."

"I doubt it," she said. "I live here and he lives in San Francisco. There's a whole lot of ocean in between. Look, I'm happy for him to see his sons and have a relationship with them. I *want* them to have a father. But when I get married I want it to be with someone who wants *me*…and not just because I'm the mother of his children."

She was about to get to her feet when the doorbell rang.

"That's probably the folks," Evie said and smiled. "They've been worried about you. Which might have something to do with the fake head cold you said you had to keep us all at bay."

"Not that it did any good," Mary-Jayne said and grinned.

"Want me to get it?" Grace asked.

"Nah," she said and pulled herself out of the soft sofa. "I got it."

She walked down the hall and opened the front door, half expecting her mother to be standing there with a big pot of chicken soup. But it wasn't either of her parents.

It was Daniel.

He looked so good. So familiar. In jeans and a blue shirt, everything about him screamed sexy and wholly masculine. She wished she was immune. She wished he didn't set her blood and skin on fire. His steely gaze traveled over her slowly until he finally met her eyes with his own and spoke.

"So you didn't run too far after all?"

"Run?"

Daniel had expected her to slam the door. But she didn't look all that surprised to see him on her doorstep.

"Your friend said you might be tempted to run to get away from me."

"Audrey did?" She laughed loudly. "I'm afraid she's got a vivid imagination and a flair for the dramatic."

"Speaking of which," Daniel said pointedly, "taking off without a word was a little theatrical, don't you think?"

She shrugged and her T-shirt slipped off her shoulder. "I needed some breathing space."

"I wasn't exactly smothering you."

"Maybe not to you," she flipped back.

He grinned a little, even though his insides churned. She had a way of doing that—a way of mixing up his emotions. He was as mad as hell with her for taking off without a word, but he wouldn't show her that. Daniel turned to briefly look at the two cars in her driveway. "You have company?"

She nodded. "My sisters."

His gaze dropped to her belly. "You told them?"

"They told me," she said, and pulled the T-shirt over her middle a fraction. "Hard to hide this from the world now."

"You shouldn't," he said quietly. "You look good."

She shrugged. "So...I guess I'll see you around."

Daniel laughed lightly. "Oh, no, Mary-Jayne, you don't get out of it that easy."

Her gaze narrowed. "You plan on camping on my doorstep?"

"If I have to," he replied. "Or you could invite me in."

His eyes widened. "You want to meet my sisters, is that it?"

"Absolutely."

She exhaled heavily and stepped back. "Okay. Best you come inside."

Daniel crossed the threshold of her small cottage and followed her down the hall. Her house was filled with old furniture and bric-a-brac and was as muddled as he'd expected. The Preston sisters regarded him curiously when he entered the living room and as Mary-Jayne introduced him. They were similar, all with the same dark curling hair and wide green eyes. Evie was down to earth and friendly, while Grace had a kind of ethereal beauty that made her look as though she'd stepped off the set of a Hollywood movie.

The eldest, Evie, asked him if he'd had a good trip and began chatting about flying and vacations, which he figured she was doing to break the ice a little. The other sister was more serious and content to stand back and watch Mary-Jayne and him interact. It didn't bother him. All he cared about was Mary-Jayne.

He cared...

Damn.

He didn't want to think about that. But he couldn't get the vision of her staring up at him in his dad's studio, her hand gently rubbing his arm, all wide-eyed and lovely. In that moment he realized she was kind and considerate, despite the bouts of exuberant bravado.

Her siblings were nice women who were clearly curious about him but were too polite to say too much. They stayed for a few minutes, and he asked about Evie's art and mentioned how his father was an artist, and she said she knew his work. Both women talked about Crystal Point and how much they loved the small town. Daniel hadn't taken much notice as he'd driven along the waterfront. His mind was set on seeing Mary-Jayne, not the beach. Evie suggested he drop by her bed-and-breakfast, and he noticed how Mary-Jayne scowled at her sister. Maybe he had an ally in the Preston sisters? Maybe they agreed that she should marry him? He wasn't averse to using whatever leverage he could if it meant he'd have the chance to be a full-time father to his sons.

Once they left, Mary-Jayne propped her hands on her hips and glared at him.

"I suppose you'd like coffee?"

He smiled. "If it's not too much trouble."

She tossed her incredible hair. "Oh, it is…not that it would make one damn bit of difference to you. And by the way," she said as she walked down the hall, "don't think you can sway me by charming my family. I've already told my sisters what a jerk you are."

He laughed and walked after her. "I don't think they quite believed you, Mary-Jayne."

When he reached the kitchen he stood by the counter for a moment, looking around at the crowded room with its cluttered cabinets, colorful drapes and assortment of pots hanging from hooks above the stove top. But as untidy and overdone as it was, there was something oddly welcoming about the room. With its mismatched table and chairs and the wrought iron stand in the corner jammed with an array of ceramic vases containing a variety of overgrown herbs, it was far removed from the huge ultramodern kitchen in his San Francisco apartment. He never used it these days. Even when he was married, Simone had worked long hours like he did and they preferred to dine out most evenings. But Mary-Jayne's kitchen suited her. It was easy to imagine her sitting at the round scrubbed table, sipping tea from one of the patterned china cups from the collection on the dresser.

"Yes," she said, still scowling. "I'm a slob, remember?"

"Did I say that?"

"Words to the effect. One of my many flaws."

He chuckled and watched her pull a pair of ceramic mugs from the cupboard. She looked so beautiful with her scowl, all fired up and ready to do battle with him. One thing was for sure, life with Mary-Jayne Preston sure wasn't dull!

Daniel came around the counter and stood beside her.

She turned and rested her hip against the bench, arms crossed.

"Yes?"

"Nothing," he said and reached for her, curling his hand gently around her neck.

"Don't you dare," she said, but didn't move.

"What are you so afraid of?" he asked, urging her closer. "That I'm going to kiss you? Or that you'll like it?"

"Neither," she said on a shallow breath. "Both."

"You never have to be afraid of me, Mary-Jayne," he said quietly, bringing her against him. The feel of her belly and breasts instantly spiked his libido. "I'd never hurt you. Or make you to do something you didn't want to do."

"Then, stop asking me to marry you," she said, still breathless as she looked up into his face.

"I can't. When I want something I'm—"

"Relentless," she said, cutting off his words. "Yeah, I know. I'm not used to someone like you," she admitted, her mouth trembling a little. "My last boyfriend was—"

"An unemployed musician," he finished for her, not in the mood to hear about the man she'd once dated. "Yes, I had you investigated, remember?"

She frowned and wriggled against him. "Jerk."

Daniel moved his other arm around her waist and gently held her. "Me or him?"

"You."

He chuckled. "You know, I don't think you really mean that."

"Sure I do," she said, and wriggled some more. "And kissing me isn't going to get me to change my mind."

"Maybe not," he said and dipped his head. "But it sure beats arguing about it."

Her lips were soft when he claimed them. Soft and sweet and familiar. Her hands crept up his chest and reached his shoulders and she clung on to him. Daniel pressed closer and she moaned softly. The sweet vanilla scent that was uniquely hers assailed his senses, and he tilted her head a fraction. Their tongues met and danced. And he was pretty sure she knew exactly the effect she had on him and his libido. His hand moved down to her hip, and he urged her closer. Heat flared between them, and suddenly kissing wasn't enough. Her fingertips dug into his shoulders and she arched her back, drawing them closer together.

"Mary-Jayne," he whispered against her mouth and trailed his lips down her cheek and throat. "Let me stay with you tonight."

She shivered in his arms. "I can't," she said on a shallow breath. "Tomorrow..."

"Forget tomorrow," he said, and pushed the T-shirt off her shoulder. Her creamy skin was like tonic for the desire that churned through his blood. "Forget everything but right now."

It was what he wanted. What he needed. Her skin, her mouth, her tender touch. He'd shut off from truly feeling anything for so long, but Mary-Jayne made him feel in ways he could barely understand. They fought; they battled with words and with ideals. But underneath the conflict simmered an attraction and a pull that was the most powerful of his life.

And it also had the power to undo him.

Chapter Eight

She didn't let him stay. She couldn't. If he'd stayed and they'd made love she wasn't sure she would have had the strength to refuse his marriage proposal. He'd use sex to confuse and manipulate her, even if that wasn't his intention. She was like putty in his arms. One kiss, one touch and being with him was all she could think about.

Idiot...

Mary-Jayne garnered all her strength and sent him packing. And tried to convince herself she couldn't care less where he went. There were plenty of quality hotels in the nearby town of Bellandale. It was barely a twenty-minute drive from Crystal Point. He had a GPS. He'd be fine. She didn't feel bad at all.

She had a shower, made soup and toast and curled up on the sofa to watch TV with Pricilla and pretended she'd put Daniel out of her mind once and for all.

Her dreams, however, were something else altogether.

He invaded them. She couldn't keep him out. His touch was like a brand against her skin, and she could still feel the heat of his body pressed against her for hours later. And his kiss... It was like no other. She remembered his comment about her ex-boyfriend. *An unemployed musician?* Toby had been exactly that. He wasn't even much of a musician. They'd dated off and on for two years and she often wondered if she'd brought home a tattooed, frequently pierced, dreadlocked boyfriend simply because that was what everyone expected of her. Her teenage willfulness made her rebel against what she'd considered the average or mundane. After she'd left home she'd saved her money and quickly headed overseas. She'd returned feeling even more independent and more determined to live her own life.

And Toby was the end result. A deadbeat, she realized now. Someone who took advantage of her generous nature and swindled her out of her money and her pride. She'd been left with a debt for a car he crashed and a guitar he'd taken with him when he walked out the door. He had no goals, no ambition and no integrity. She'd had one serious relationship since with a man who ended up complaining about her spending too much time worrying about her career. He'd had no ambition, either—except the desire to sit in front of his computer all day playing games. She'd foolishly believed she chose men who were free-spirited and artistic. Now they simply seemed lazy and immature.

She tossed and turned all night and woke up feeling nauseated and unable to stomach the dry crackers and green tea that usually helped most when morning sickness came upon her.

She changed into her favorite overalls and grinned when she discovered she had to leave two of the three side buttons undone to accommodate her rapidly expanding middle. Her workshop needed a cleanup before she got to work on the few back orders she had, so she headed outside and began decluttering the counters. It was midmorning before she took a break and snacked on some apple slices and a cup of tea.

At eleven Daniel rocked up.

In dark jeans and a navy polo shirt he looked effortlessly handsome, and her stomach flipped with familiar awareness. He looked her over and smiled.

"Cute outfit."

Her overalls were paint splattered and had holes in each knee. But they were comfy, and she could care less what he thought about her clothes. "Thanks. Did you want something?" she asked, pushing the memory of his kisses from her mind.

"We're going out."

Bossy, as usual. "Are we? Am I allowed to ask where we're going?"

"To see your parents," he said swiftly. "It's about time they were told they're about to become grandparents again."

"I'd rather tell them myself."

"*We'll* tell them," he said, firmer this time. "Stop being stubborn."

Mary-Jayne turned and sashayed down the hall. "I'd really prefer to do it some other time. Please try to understand."

"Well, I don't. We're in this together," he said, and followed her into the house. "We told my parents together… and now we'll tell yours…together. That's how things are going to be, Mary-Jayne. They have a right to know, don't you think?"

When she reached the living room she turned and

propped her hands on her hips. "Of course. I just don't want you to meet them right now."

His brows shot up. "Why the hell not?"

"Because," she said, and dragged out a long breath, "you don't know them. One look at you and they'll get all...thingy."

He stilled. *"Thingy?"*

Her patience frayed. "Excited, okay? Thrilled. Happy. They'll feel as though they've won the lottery in the potential son-in-law department."

He laughed. "They want you to nab a rich husband?"

"No," she corrected. "That's not it. It's just that you're different from anyone I've ever...you know...dated. You're not an *unemployed musician*," she explained, coloring hotly. "Or a beach bum or a lazy good-for-nothing, as my dad would say. You're...*normal*... You're successful and hardworking and come from a nice family. Once they know that, they'll get all worked up and start pressuring me to...to..."

"Marry me?"

"Well, yeah," she admitted. "Probably."

"I thought you said they let you lead your own life?"

"They do," she replied. "But they're still my parents. They still want what's best for me. Once they clap eyes on you, I'll be done for."

His mouth twitched at the edges. "Best you get changed so we can get going."

Mary-Jayne frowned. "Didn't you hear what I said?"

"Every word," he said, and dropped into the sofa. "Hurry up, *dear*."

Impatience snaked up her spine. "You are the most infuriating and—"

"Want me to kiss you again?" he asked as he grabbed a

magazine from the coffee table and opened it at a random page. "If not, go and get changed."

Irritated, she turned on her heels and stomped to her bedroom. He was an ass. He didn't give a hoot what she wanted. Or care about how she felt. By the time she'd dressed, Mary-Jayne was so mad she could have slugged his smug face.

Once they were out of the house she pointed to her car. "I'll drive," she said and rattled her keys. "I know the way."

Daniel stopped midstride and looked at the battered VW in the driveway. "In that hunk of junk? I don't think so." He gestured to the top-of-the-range Ford sedan parked alongside the curb. "We'll take my rental car."

"Snob."

He laughed and gently grasped her elbow. "Come on."

"Sometimes I really don't like you much at all."

He laughed again. "And other times?"

She quickstepped it to the car and waited by the passenger door. It was hard to stay mad at him when he was being so nice to her. "No comment."

Once they were in the car she gave him the address. The trip took only minutes, and by the time they pulled into the driveway her temper had lost its momentum.

"You're something of a hothead, aren't you?" he asked as he unclipped his seat belt.

"Around you?" She raised a brow and smiled a little. "Yeah."

He seemed to find that idea amusing and was still chuckling by the time he was out of the car and had come around to her side. "It's one of the things I find captivating about you, Mary-Jayne."

Captivating? That was quite an admission. He usually didn't admit to anything, not when it came to feelings. Oh, sure, she knew he wanted her in his bed, but anything else seemed off his agenda. He'd said he felt numb. The very idea pained her deep down. He'd lost the woman he'd loved and didn't want to love again... That was clear enough.

"What are you thinking about?" he asked as he took her hand.

I'm thinking about how it must feel to be loved by you...

Mary-Jayne's fingers tingled at the connection with his. She didn't want to be so vulnerable to his touch, but her attraction for him had a will of its own. She simply couldn't help herself. That was why she'd become so caught up in the heat and passion between them the night of Solana's birthday party. It was heady and powerful and drove her beyond coherent thought. It was more than attraction. More than anything she'd felt before.

And the very idea scared her senseless.

Her parents, as expected, were delighted, if not a little shocked at their news. Once the shock settled, her mother had countless questions for Daniel and he answered every one without faltering. He was as resilient as the devil when under intense scrutiny. Barbara Preston skirted around the question about marriage and Mary-Jayne was relieved that Daniel didn't mention that she'd refused his proposal. There was time for that revelation later. Her father, she realized, looked as pleased as she'd ever seen him. Bill Preston approved. Daniel was a hit. Her parents were clearly delighted, even with her out-of-wedlock pregnancy. Her mother was all hugs and tears when they explained she was expecting twins.

Over a jug of iced tea her father spoke. "What do you think of our little town, son?"

Son?

Her dad was already calling Daniel "son"?

Great.

"I haven't had a chance to see much of it yet," Daniel

replied. "But I'm hoping Mary-Jayne will show me around sometime today."

She smiled sweetly and nodded, and then noticed how her mother seemed to approve wholeheartedly about the way Daniel used her full name. He could clearly do no wrong.

I'm doomed.

They stayed for two hours, and Daniel answered every probing question her parents asked. He talked about his career, his family and even his wife and the baby they had lost. Before they left her father ushered him off to his garage to inspect the Chevrolet Impala that he was restoring, and Mary-Jayne was left to endure her mother's scrutiny.

"Now," Barbara said, hugging her closely once the men had left the room. "What don't I know?"

"Nothing," she replied and began collecting the mugs from the table. "The babies are doing fine and I feel okay other than a little morning sickness."

"I meant with the two of you," Barbara said and raised a brow. "He's awfully handsome, isn't he? And such nice manners."

Mary-Jayne smiled. "I know he isn't what you've imagined I'd bring home to meet you."

"Well, your track record hasn't exactly given us confidence."

"I know. And you're right—he's handsome and nice and has good manners."

"Are you in love with him?"

Love...

She'd not considered the word in regard to him. Falling in love with Daniel was out of the question. He'd never love her back. *He was numb.* There was nothing left in his heart. He'd love their sons and that was all.

"No," she said and heard the hesitation in her own voice. "Definitely not."

Barbara smiled. "It wouldn't be the end of the world, you know... I mean, if you did fall in love with a man like Daniel."

"It would," she corrected, suddenly hurting deep in her chest. "He still loves his wife. And she was very different from me. She was smart and successful and everything I'm not."

There...I said it out loud.

Her mother's expression softened some more. "You're smart, and your dad and I have every faith that your business will be a success one day. And sometimes being *different* is a good thing," Barbara added gently.

"Not in this," she said, her heart suddenly and inexplicably heavy. "I know you only want to see me happy, and I am happy about the babies. Really happy. Even though it's been something of a shock I'm looking forward to being a mother."

Barbara rubbed her arm comfortingly. "You'll be a good one, too, I'm sure of it."

"I hope so," she said. "Although I'm sure some people will think having twin boys is my medicine for being such a difficult child myself."

Her mother smiled. "You were spirited, not difficult."

"That's sweet of you to say so, but I know I caused you and Dad some major headaches over the years. Remember when I ditched school for three days to follow that carnival that had arrived in town?"

Barbara laughed. "Every kid dreams of running away and joining the circus at some point. Especially a strong-willed eleven-year-old."

Mary-Jayne giggled. "I had visions of being a trapeze artist."

They chatted for a few more minutes about her childhood escapades, and by the time her father and Daniel returned her mood was much improved. Daniel looked his usual self-satisfied self and her dad looked pleased as punch. Whatever had transpired in the garage, she was sure it had something to do her father giving Daniel his blessing and full support.

Typical...

Once they were back in the car, she strapped on the seat belt and pasted on a smile.

"Take a left at the end of the street," she instructed.

"Because?"

"You wanted to see my town, my home, right?"

"Well...yes."

"So we'll go to the beach."

He frowned a little. "We're not exactly dressed for the beach."

Mary-Jayne laughed. "Does everything always have to be done to order with you? Live dangerously, Daniel," she said and laughed again. "You might surprise yourself and enjoy it."

His mouth tightened. "You know, despite what you think, I'm not some overworked killjoy."

"Prove it," she challenged. "Get those extrastarched clothes of yours crumpled for a moment."

"Extrastarched?" he echoed as he started the ignition.

She chuckled. "Oh, come on, even you have to admit that you're a neat freak. You even folded your clothes that night we spent together." It was something of an exaggeration...but she had a point to prove. "My dress got twisted amongst the bedsheets and your suit was perfectly placed over the chair."

"I don't remember it that way."

"Hah," she scoffed. "You have a selective memory."

"I remember everything about that night," he said and drove down the street. "Left, you said?"

"Left," she repeated. "We'll drive past my sister's bed-and-breakfast."

"I know where that is already."

Her brows came up. "You do?"

He nodded. "Of course. I stayed there last night."

Daniel knew it would make her nuts. But he'd thought it was a good idea at the time and Evie Jones seemed to agree. After Mary-Jayne had kicked him out of her house the evening before, he'd driven around the small town for a while and come across Dunn Inn by chance. The big A-framed house stood silhouetted amongst a nest of Norfolk pines and the shingle out front had told him exactly who the place belonged to. So he'd tapped on the door and was met by Evie's much younger husband, Scott, and within minutes Evie herself was insisting he stay at the bed-and-breakfast while he was in Crystal Point.

"You stayed at my sister's place?"

She was all outraged, and it made him grin a little. "Sure. Something wrong with that?"

"Something? Everything! Of all the manipulative and conniving things I could imagine you—"

"I needed somewhere to stay," he said quickly. "You told me to leave, remember?"

"Ever heard of a thing called a hotel?" she shot back. "There are many of them in Bellandale."

"I wanted to stay in Crystal Point."

"Why?"

He glanced at her belly. "You have to ask?"

She glared at him. "Don't use the twins as a way of getting around this. How long do you intend on staying?"

"As long as I need to."

"You could stay for a lifetime and nothing would change. I will not marry you. Not now and not ever."

"We'll see," he said, with way more confidence than he felt.

The truth was, he was tired of arguing with her about it. She was as stubborn as a mule. Last night he could have stayed with her. He'd wanted to. A part of him had needed to. He'd wanted to spend the night making love to her. And her rejection had stung like a bucket of ice water over his skin.

"What about your job?" she asked. "You can't just pack that in for an indeterminable length of time."

"Sure I can," he said, and flipped a lazy smile and drove toward the beach. "I'm the boss, remember? I can do what I want."

She was clearly fuming. "Solana told me you never take vacations."

"This isn't a vacation," he said, and pulled the car into the parking area.

"No," she said, opening the door. "It's a hunting expedition…and I'm the prey."

Daniel got out of the car, ignoring the niggling pain in his temple. "Such drama. Let's just forget my marriage proposal for the moment, shall we?"

"It's all I can think about," she muttered.

"Well, that's something, at least." He locked the car. "So this beach?"

She crossed her arms and stormed off down the pathway. Daniel had to admit the beach was spectacular. The white sand spanned for several hundred meters until it met the pristine river mouth. No wonder she loved this place so much. It was early winter and a weekday, so there was no one about other than them and a lone dog walker playing chase with his pet. He watched as Mary-Jayne flipped off her sandals and strode across the sand until she reached the water. Daniel looked down at his shoes. They were Italian leather and not designed for the beach. He perched on a rock and took them off, stuffing the socks into the loafers. She'd called him an uptight neat freak on several occasions. Maybe she was right. When he was young he'd been impulsive and adventurous. Now he rarely did anything without considering the consequences. Taking over the helm of Anderson's from his grandfather had changed him. He felt the weight of responsibility press heavily on his shoulders 24/7. The most impulsive thing he'd done recently was go after Mary-Jayne. And even that he did with a tempered spirit. What he really wanted to do was haul her in his arms and kiss her senseless.

By the time he stepped onto the sand she was twenty meters in front of him. He quickened his steps and watched her as she walked, mesmerized by the way her hips swayed. She had a sensuality that affected him in a way that blurred the lines between desire and something else. Something more. He couldn't define it. Couldn't articulate in his mind what it was about Mary-Jayne that caused such an intense reaction in him. It wasn't simply attraction. He'd felt that before and it had always waned quickly. No, this was something he'd never experienced before. Not even with Simone. His wife hadn't driven him crazy. Loving her had been easy. She had never challenged him, insulted him or made him accountable for his beliefs. But Mary-Jayne did at every opportunity. She questioned everything and anything.

She made him think.

Feel...

It was a kind of heady mix of torture and pleasure.

Which was why making love with her had been so intense. They had chemistry and more. A connection that went beyond physical attraction. A mental attraction that defied logic.

Yeah, loving Simone had been easy. But loving Mary-Jayne… There would be nothing easy about that. Which was why he wouldn't. Why he'd keep it clear in his head what he wanted. His sons. A family. But where? It could never be here, he thought as he walked along the sand. Sure, it was a nice town. Peaceful and safe… Exactly the kind of place to raise children. The kind of place a person could call home. But not him. For one, Mary-Jayne would never agree to it. And he had his life in San Francisco.

She was walking at a leisurely pace now and stopped to pick something up, perhaps a shell. Daniel caught up with her and matched her slow strides.

"It's a beautiful spot."

She glanced sideways. "It's the prettiest beach along this part of the coastline."

"You're fortunate to have grown up in a place like this. To have made it your home."

She shrugged and tossed the shell in the shallow water. "What about you?" she asked. "Where's home for you?"

Daniel rubbed the back of his neck to ease the tension creeping up his spine. "San Francisco."

"That's where you live," she said quietly. "Where's home?"

He shrugged loosely. "When my grandfather was alive he and Solana had a place in the Napa Valley, and I used to go there for school vacations. Miles and Bernie moved around a lot, so my brothers and I always welcomed the stability of my grandparents' small vineyard. But when Gramps died things changed. Gran wasn't interested in the business end of things and decided to sell the place. Solana likes the warmer weather and divides her time between Port Douglas and San Francisco."

She stopped walking and faced him, her hair flipping around her face from the breeze. "So…nowhere?"

"I guess so," he replied, and started walking again.

She caught up with him quickly. "I don't want that for my babies. I want them to be settled. I want them to have a place they can always call home."

"So do I," he said, and stopped to look out over the water. "What's that called?" he asked, pointing to a land mass separated from the shore by an expanse of water that fed from the mouth of the river.

"Jays Island," she replied. "Years ago they used to bring sugarcane ferries up the river, so this was quite a busy spot. Now they use trains and trucks to transport the sugar so the river doesn't get dredged anymore. The sand banks built up and the island came about. Birds nest over there and at a really low tide you can wade through the shallows to get over there. When I was young I used to swim over there at high tide and come back when the tide went out." She laughed and the sound flittered across the wind. "Much to my parents' despair. But I loved sitting on that patch of rock," she said, and pointed to a ragged rock outcrop on the island. "I used to sit there for ages and just let the wind hit my face. It was the kind of place where a person could dream big and no one was around to make judgment. Where *I* could sit without worrying about other people's opinion."

"You mean your family?"

She shrugged. "My family are the best."

"But?"

Her green eyes glittered. "But everyone has a role, you know… My brother, my sisters. Noah took over the family business, Evie's the successful artist, Grace is the supersmart financial whiz who once worked on Wall Street."

"And you?"

Her shoulders lifted again. "I'm just the youngest. The one who got away with everything as a kid. I guess I have the role of being the one who hasn't amounted to anything."

Surely she didn't believe that. "A college education and a big bank balance don't equate to a person's value, Mary-Jayne. There's greatness in simply being yourself."

She offered a wry smile. "Is that why you've worked so hard to climb the corporate ladder? Because you believe it's enough to live a simple life?"

"An authentic life," he corrected, doing his best to ignore the growing throb in his head. "But I didn't really have a choice when I was drafted into the company. My dad wasn't interested, and my grandfather had a lot of health issues. I either joined or the company folded. Too many people were invested in Anderson's... I couldn't let it go down without a fight. So I made a few changes to the company's structure, sold off most of the mining interests and concentrated on the part that I enjoyed. Ten years later the resorts are now some of the most successful in the world."

"And if you hadn't joined the family business, what would you have done?"

"I'm not sure. Maybe law."

She laughed. "Oh, yes, I can see you as a lawyer. You do pose a good argument."

He reached out and grabbed her left hand, and then gently rubbed her ring finger with his thumb. "Not good enough, obviously. This is still bare."

She went to pull away but he held on. "You know why I won't."

"Because you hate me."

She shook her head. "I don't hate you, Daniel."

"No?" he queried as he turned her hand over and stroked her palm. "But you don't like me."

"I don't *dislike* you," she said quietly. "The truth is, I'm very confused about how I do feel about you. And it's not something I'm used to. Normally I know exactly how I feel about everything. I have an opinion and I usually express it. But around you…" Her words trailed. "Around you all I seem to do is dig myself into this hole and say things I don't mean. And I'm not like that. It's not a reaction I'm particularly proud of."

"So I wind you up," he said, still holding her, even though the pain in his head gained momentum. "We wind one another up. What's wrong with that? It'll keep things interesting."

"What things? A marriage where we're always fighting, always at each other's throats? That's not something I want our children to witness." She pulled away and crossed her arms tightly around her waist. "Because if you do, that's about as selfish and self-destructive as it gets."

Selfish? Selfish because he wanted to give his sons his name and the legacy that went along with it. She was the one being selfish—thinking only of herself. Like a spoiled brat.

"If you had any consideration for their future, for what they deserve, then you would see that I'm right," he said stiffly. "But right now you're acting like a petulant child, Mary-Jayne. Maybe this isn't what either of us planned. And maybe you're right, maybe we would never have seen one another again after that night if you hadn't gotten pregnant. But you did, and we are and I'll be damned if I'm going to let you dictate the kind of father I'm allowed to be. This might be a shock to you, but you're *not* the center of the universe, and right now the only thing that matters is the welfare of our sons."

She glared at him. "You're calling *me* self-absorbed? When you think you can simply snap your fingers and get what you want?"

Annoyance swept over his skin. He tried to keep his cool. Tried to get her to show some sense. But be damned if she wasn't the most infuriating woman on the planet!

In that moment a flashing light appeared out of the corner of his eye. And another. A dreaded and familiar ache clutched the back of his head. He recognized what was coming.

"We have to get back. I'll take you home."

And he knew, as he turned and walked back up the sand, that he was in for one hell of a headache.

Chapter Nine

Two days later Mary-Jayne got a call from her sister Evie. She'd had a peaceful two days. No Daniel. No marriage proposals. No insults. It gave her time to seethe and think and work.

"I think you should get over here."

She ground her teeth together. She didn't want to see him. She was still mad at him for calling her a petulant child. And she certainly didn't want her sister interfering or trying to play matchmaker. "What for?"

"He's been holed up in his room for forty-eight hours. No food or coffee or anything. I don't want to pry...but I thought you should know."

Mary-Jayne pushed down the concern battering around in her head. "He's a big boy. I'm sure he's fine."

"Well, I'm not so sure. And I have an obligation to my guests to ensure their welfare while they stay here."

"Good... You go and check on him."

"M.J.," Evie said, sterner this time. "Whatever is going on between the two of you, put it aside for a moment. *I* need your help."

Unable to refuse her sister's plea, Mary-Jayne quickly got dressed and headed over to the B and B. Evie looked genuinely concerned when she met her by the side door.

"So what's the big emergency?" she asked as she walked into the house and dropped her tote on the kitchen counter. "Maybe he's gone out."

"He's here," Evie said. "His rental car is outside."

"Maybe he's asleep."

"For two days?" her sister shot back. "Something's not right, and since you're the soon-to-be mother of his babies, it's your responsibility to find out what's wrong."

"I think you're under the illusion that Daniel and I have some kind of real relationship. We don't," Mary-Jayne informed her. "We barely tolerate one another."

Evie placed a key in her palm, touched her shoulders and gave her a little sisterly shove. "Go and find out. He's in the brown room."

There were four guest rooms at the B and B, each one styled in a particular color. Mary-Jayne left the family residence area and headed into the bigger section of the house. She lingered outside the door for a moment and finally tapped. Nothing. She tapped again.

She was about to bail when she heard a faint sound. Like a moan.

Did he have a woman in there?

The very idea made her sick to the stomach. He wouldn't...surely.

She stared at the key in her hand. What if she opened the door and found him doing who knows what with some random woman? She wouldn't be able to bear it.

Suck it up...

She pushed the key in the lock and slowly opened the door. The room was in darkness. The heavy drapes were shut and she couldn't hear a sound. There was someone on the bed, lying facedown.

"Daniel?"

She said his name so softly she wasn't surprised he didn't respond. She closed the door and stepped closer. He was naked from the waist up and had a pillow draped over his head. She said his name again and the pillow moved.

"What?"

His voice was hoarse. Groggy. Nothing like she'd heard before. She squinted to accustom her eyes to the darkness and spotted an empty bottle of aspirin on the bedside table. She took notice of everything, and a thought popped into her head.

"Are you drunk?"

He groaned softly. "Go away."

"You're hungover?"

He rolled slightly and took the pillow with him, facing away from her. "Leave me alone, Mary-Jayne."

She walked around the bed and looked at him. "Daniel, I was only wondering if—"

"I'm not drunk," he said raggedly, clearly exasperated. "I've got a headache. Now go away."

She glanced around the room. Total darkness. He hadn't eaten for two days. Empty painkiller bottle. She got to the edge of the bed and dropped to her haunches.

"Daniel," she said gently, and tried to move the pillow. "Do you have a migraine headache?"

He moaned and his hold on the pillow tightened. "Yes. Get out of here."

She got to her feet and headed into the bathroom, emerging a minute later with a cold, wet washcloth. He hadn't moved. She sat on the edge of the bed.

"Here," she said, and pried the pillow off him. "This will help." She gently rolled him onto his back and placed the cloth across his forehead.

"Stop fussing," he said croakily.

She pressed the cloth around his temples. "Let me help you."

"You can't."

"I can," she said and touched his hair. "My mother gets migraines. I know what I'm doing." She glanced at the empty medicine bottle. "When did you last take a pain-killer?"

He shrugged and then moaned, as though the movement took all his effort. "This morning. Last night. I can't remember."

She stroked his head. "Okay. I'll be back soon. Keep the cloth on your forehead."

Mary-Jayne was back in a matter of minutes. Evie had what she needed, and when she returned to his room she noticed he was still lying on his back and had his hand over his eyes. She fetched a glass of water from the bathroom and sat on the bed again.

"Take these for now," she instructed, and pressed a couple of aspirin into his hand. "And I have some paracetamol you can take in two hours."

"Would you stop—"

"Take the pills, okay?" she said, holding on to her patience. "You'll feel better for it." He grumbled again but finally did as she requested. Mary-Jayne took the glass and placed it on the bedside table. "It's important that you take in plenty of fluids."

"Yes, nurse."

"And drop the attitude for a while."

He didn't respond. Instead he rolled over and buried his face into the pillow. Mary-Jayne got up and pushed the drapes together as close as they would go. She knew many migraine sufferers had sensitivity to light. Countless times she'd watched her mother battle for days on end with the nausea and blinding pain.

She stayed with him for the next few hours. She gave him water and made him take some more medication. When she thought he could handle it, she sat on the bed and gently massaged lavender oil into his temples. There was a strong level of intimacy in what she did, but she couldn't let him suffer.

By late afternoon there was significant improvement in his pain level, and she left for a while to make him a sandwich and peppermint tea.

"How's the patient?" Evie asked when she came into the kitchen.

Mary-Jayne looked up from her task. "A little better. He's hungry, so that's a good sign."

Evie nodded and grinned. "Yeah... You were right—you two don't have a relationship at all. What was I thinking?"

"I'm helping someone who's in pain, that's all."

"That someone is the father of your babies. It's a bond, M.J. A strong bond that will forever keep you and Daniel in each other's life."

"I know it will," she said, heavyhearted. "I just don't know why he keeps insisting that we get married."

Evie raised her brows in dramatic fashion. "He lost a child once... I think it's easy to understand why he doesn't want to lose his sons, too."

"Lose them to what?" she shot back.

"Geography," Evie replied. "An ocean between you is a big incentive. Or the idea you might meet someone else one day and get married."

She wasn't about to admit she'd deliberately avoided considering any of that before.

"Marriage without love could never work."

"Are you sure about that?" Evie queried. "I mean, are you sure there's no love there? Looks to me as if you're behaving exactly like a woman in love would act."

She stilled instantly. Her sister's words rattled around in her head.

No, it wasn't true. She didn't. She couldn't.

"I'm not," she said, defiant.

Evie smiled gently. "I've never known you to be afraid of anything. What is it about loving this man that scares you so much?"

Nothing. Everything. Her sister was way too intuitive. "He's out of my league."

"Why? Because he has short hair and a job?"

The reference to her ex-boyfriend didn't go unmissed. "We're too different. And he'll want to shuffle me off to San Francisco. I don't want to live there. I want to live here. But he'll do and say whatever he has to in order to get his own way. I know he's handsome and can be charming and ticks all the boxes. But I know him... He's a control freak."

"So are you, in your own way," Evie remarked. "So maybe you're not so different after all."

Was that it? Was it their similarities and not their differences that spooked her? He'd called her a hothead. She'd called him arrogant. Were they both guilty of those traits?

Mary-Jayne ignored the idea for the moment and grabbed the tray. "I have to get back in there."

Evie smiled. "See you a little later."

When she returned to his room the bed was empty. The curtains were still drawn and there was a sliver of light beaming from beneath the closed bathroom door. He came out moments later, naked except for a towel draped around his hips, another towel in his hand that he used to dry his hair.

She pushed down the rush of blood in her veins. But his shoulders were so wide, his chest broad and dusted with a smattering of hair and his stomach as flat as a washboard that the picture was wholly masculine. A deep surge of longing flowed through her.

"You're back."

She swallowed hard and tried to not look at his smooth skin. "I'm back," she said, and placed the tray on the small table by the window. "How are you feeling?"

"Weary," he said, and smiled fractionally as he came toward her. "It takes me a few days to come good after."

Mary-Jayne poured some tea and made a determined effort to stop looking at him as if he was a tasty meal. "Have you always suffered from migraines?" she asked, eyes downcast.

He nodded. "Since I was a kid. They're less frequent now, but when one hits I usually just lock myself in my apartment with some aspirin for a couple of days and try to sleep it off."

"Have you tried stronger medication? Perhaps an injection of—"

"No needles," he said, and moved beside her.

He smelled so good. Like soap and some musky deodorant. She swallowed hard and glanced sideways. The towel hitched around his hips had slipped a little. "I should let you have some privacy and—"

"Shy?" he queried, reading her thoughts effortlessly. "It's nothing you haven't seen before."

Mary-Jayne swallowed hard. He was right. She'd seen every part of him. Touched every part of him. Been with him in the most intimate way possible. And still there was something unknown about him, something inviting and extraordinarily sexy. There was nothing overt about Daniel. He wasn't one of those constantly charming men who flirted and manipulated. He was sexually confident but not obvious. It was one of the reasons why she found him so blindingly attractive. He could have her as putty in his hands if he wanted to, but he didn't try to sway her with sex. For sure, he'd kissed her a couple of times, but even then he'd held back. When they'd been kissing in her kitchen days earlier and she'd told him to go, he hadn't lingered. He hadn't tried to persuade her or coerce. Because he possessed, she realized, bucketloads of integrity.

"You know," she said bluntly as she stirred the tea, "if you kissed me right now you'd probably have me in that bed in less than two seconds."

He chuckled. "I know."

"Except for your migraine, of course."

"I wouldn't let a lousy headache get in the way."

His words made her insides jump. She poured a second mug of tea and sat down. "Shall I open the curtains?" she asked, noticing that the only light in the room was coming from the direction of the open bathroom door. "Or are you still too sensitive?"

"I'm okay now."

She pushed the drapes aside a little. "My mother can't bear light when she has an attack. My dad usually bundles her in the car and takes her to the doctor for a pain-killer injection."

He flinched. "Bernie used to try acupuncture rather than meds when I was young to combat the worst of the pain."

"Did it work?"

He shrugged loosely and sat in the chair opposite. "At times. Thank you for the tea and…everything else today."

"No problem. Glad I could help."

He sniffed the air. "I can smell flowers."

She grinned. "It's lavender oil," she explained. "I massaged some of it into your temples. It's something my dad does for my mother."

He rubbed his forehead. "Oh…well, thanks. It helped."

She sipped her tea and pushed the sandwich toward him. "You really should eat something."

He nodded and picked up the bread. "How are *you* feeling? Any nausea today?"

"No," she replied. "I've been okay for the past couple of days." She rubbed her belly and smiled. "And it's a small price to pay for having these two growing inside me."

He regarded her thoughtfully. "You're really happy about being pregnant, aren't you?"

"Ecstatic," she said and smiled. "I mean, it's not what I'd planned…but then again, I don't ever really plan anything. My work, my travels… It's always been a little ad hoc. But now I can feel them, I know I couldn't be happier."

"Except for the fact that I'm their father?" he queried, one brow raised.

Mary-Jayne met his gaze. "I've never wished for it to be any different. I think you'll be a really great dad." She sighed heavily. "And I get it, you know…about why you want to get married. You didn't get a chance, last time, to be a father. That was taken away from you. But I would never do anything to keep you from your sons, Daniel. They're a part of you, just like they're a part of me."

His gray eyes smoldered. "So you think all that, and you still won't marry me."

"No."

He tossed the untouched sandwich back onto the tray. "Okay. I won't ask you again."

It was what she wanted. No more proposals. No more pursuit. But somehow, in the back of her mind, she felt a strange sensation. Like…like disappointment. But she managed a tight smile. "Thank you."

"And custody?"

"We can share it. Of course, I'm going to live here and you'll be in San Francisco…but you can see them whenever you want."

"Don't you think that will confuse them?" he asked quietly. "Me randomly turning up to play daddy."

"At first," she said, and gritted her back teeth. "But it's going to be impossible to share custody when we live in two different countries."

"They could live here for six months and then in San Francisco for six months."

Fear snaked up her spine. "You wouldn't?"

"I wouldn't what?"

Mary-Jayne perched herself on the edge of the chair. "Try to get fifty percent custody. I couldn't bear to be away from them for six months at a time. I know you've got money enough to get the best lawyers, but I really couldn't—"

"You misunderstand, Mary-Jayne," he said, cutting her off. "I meant you and the twins could live in San Francisco for six months. Look, I know you love this town and don't want to be away from it permanently, but perhaps we could meet in the middle, metaphorically speaking. I'll buy you a house near where I live and you could settle there every six months."

"You'll *buy* me a house? Just like that?"

He shrugged. "Sure."

"And fly me and the twins back and forth every six months?"

"Yes."

Meet in the middle? Perhaps that was the only way to settle the tension between them. And as much as she protested, she knew she'd do whatever she had to do if it meant retaining full custody of her babies. "We'll see what happens. Anyhow," she said and got to her feet, "you should rest for a while. You look like you need it."

"Can I see you later?"

"No," she replied. "You need to get some sleep. And I have some work to do. I'm making some pieces for a friend of Solana's and I need to concentrate."

"My grandmother is very fond of you," he said, and got to his feet. The towel slipped a little more and she averted her gaze. It wasn't good for her self-control to keep staring at his bare chest.

"I'm fond of her, too."

"I know," he said, and then added more soberly, "and I apologize if I might have suggested you were not pure in your motives when you got to know her. She told me you turned down her offer to finance your business. I should trust her judgment... She knows people way better than I do."

Heat crawled up her neck. He was paying her a compliment. It shouldn't have embarrassed her, but it did. "I understand you only wanted to protect her. But I genuinely like Solana and would never take advantage of her in any way."

"I know that, Mary-Jayne. But if you need help getting your business off the ground, then I would be more than—"

"No," she said and raised a hand. "My business is mediocre because I'm not all that ambitious... I never have been. I like designing and crafting the pieces, but that's where my interest ends. I started selling them online almost by mistake. My friends Lauren and Cassie persuaded me to start a website showcasing the things I'd made and then all of a sudden I had orders coming in. I do it because

I have to make a living doing something, and why not earn money doing what I enjoy creatively."

He nodded as if he understood. She'd expected him to try to sway her some more, but to his credit he accepted her explanation. "I'll see you soon, then."

"Okay," she said, and shrugged lightly, even though the idea of spending more time with him tied her insides into knots. She liked him. A lot. And that made it increasingly difficult to keep him at arm's length. "I hope you feel better."

It took another two days for Daniel to get back to his normal self. He conference called his brothers to keep up with business and spoke to his grandmother. Solana was keen to know the details of his visit with Mary-Jayne, but he didn't tell her much. He certainly wasn't going to admit she'd turned him down again and again.

On Friday morning he headed to the kitchen and found Evie elbow-deep in some kind of baking.

"Good morning," she greeted, and smiled. "Coffee?"

He nodded and helped himself to a mug and half filled it with coffee. "Cooking for the masses?" he asked as he looked over the large bowls in front of her before he perched himself on a stool by the counter.

"For the fire station," she said cheerfully. "My husband, Scott, is a fireman. He's on night shift at the moment and I usually bake a few dozen cupcakes to keep him and the rest of the crew going."

It was a nice gesture, he thought. A loving gesture. "He's a lucky guy."

She smiled. "I'm the lucky one. He moved here, you know, from California. He'd come here for his sister's wedding to my older brother and we fell in love, but he left a few weeks after he arrived. When I discovered I was pregnant he came back and stayed. He knew I could never leave here... I had a teenage son and my family. So he changed his life for me. It was a very selfless gesture."

Daniel didn't miss the meaning of her words.

But live in Crystal Point permanently? He couldn't. It wasn't the place for him. He had a business to run. He couldn't do that from a tiny town that was barely a spot on the map. Plus, he had a life in San Francisco. Friends. Routine. A past. He'd known Simone there. Loved her there. Grieved her there. To leave would be like abandoning those feelings. And Mary-Jayne had made her thoughts abundantly clear. He was pretty sure she didn't want him anywhere near her precious town. That was why he'd suggested she come to San Francisco for six months of the year. It was a sensible compromise. The only way around the situation.

"I'm glad it worked out for you," he said, and drank some coffee.

One of her eyebrows came up. "Things have a way of doing that, you know."

"Or they don't."

She smiled. "I like to believe that anything is possible... if you want it enough."

It was a nice idea, but he didn't really agree. He'd wanted his wife and daughter to be safe. But fate had other plans. Things happened. Bad things. Good things. Sometimes it was simply a matter of timing.

"She's always been headstrong," Evie said, and smiled again. "Don't let that bravado fool you though. Underneath she's as vulnerable as the next person."

"I know she is. She's also stubborn."

"Perhaps that's because she thinks you shouldn't always get your own way?" Evie suggested.

He laughed a little. "You might be right. But I'm not out to change her. I only want to be a father to my children."

"Maybe that's where you're going wrong," Evie said. "Maybe you need to concentrate on her first and foremost."

"Nice idea," he said ruefully. "Have you met your sister? She's not exactly giving me an opportunity."

"She's scared of you."

Daniel straightened. "Of me? Why? I'd never harm her or—"

"Of course you wouldn't," Evie said quickly. "I mean she's scared of what you represent. You're...normal... You know...not a—"

"Unemployed musician?" he finished for her. "Yeah, we've already had the ex-boyfriend discussion. She's anti-wealth, antisuccess, anti-anything that gives her a reason to keep me out of the little bubble she's wrapped in."

"It's protection, that's all. Her first boyfriend was a deadbeat who stole her money. The one after that was a lazy so-and-so. If she's with you, it's as if she's admitting that she's not who everyone thinks she is. That all the other guys were just a phase...an aberration. That she isn't really a free spirit who does what she wants. It means that she's as vulnerable to a perfectly respectable and nice man as the rest of womankind is."

Daniel laughed. "So you're saying she won't marry me because I'm not a deadbeat?"

"Precisely."

He was still thinking of Evie's words when he was in town later that morning. Bellandale was a big regional town and had sufficient offerings to get what he needed done. By the afternoon he was back in Crystal Point and pulled up outside Mary-Jayne's house around five o'clock. She was in the front garden, crouched down and pulling weeds from an overgrown herb garden. She wore bright pink overalls that showed off her lovely curves and the popped-out belly. He watched her for a moment, marveling at her effortless beauty. His insides were jumping all over the place. No one had ever confounded him as much as Mary-Jayne Preston.

She stood up when she realized there was a car by the curb. She dropped the gloves and small garden fork in her hand and came down the driveway. Her crazily beautiful hair whipped around her face.

Daniel got out of the car and closed the door. "Good afternoon."

"You look better," she said as she approached. "Headache all gone?"

"Yes. How are you feeling?"

"I'm good," she said, and came beside the car. "Nice wheels. It doesn't look like a rental."

Daniel glanced at the white BMW and rattled the keys. "It's not."

Her eyes widened. "You bought a car?"

He nodded. "I did. Do you like it?"

She shrugged. "It's nice, I suppose. Very…highbrow."

A smile tugged at his mouth. "It's a sensible family car."

She looked it over and nodded. "I suppose it is. Since you had the rental, I didn't realize you needed a car."

"I don't," he said and grabbed her hand. "I still have the rental." He opened her fingers and rested the key in her palm. "It's yours."

Her eyes instantly bulged and she stepped back. "Mine?"

He nodded. "That's right."

The moment it registered her expression sharpened. "You bought me a car?"

"I did. I thought you—"

"I have a car," she said stiffly. "And it works just fine."

Daniel glanced at the beat-up, rusted yellow Volkswagen in the driveway. "Your car is old and not roadworthy."

Her hands propped onto her hips. "How do you know that? Have you taken it for a spin around the block?"

"I don't need to," he replied. "Take a look at it."

"I like it." She stepped forward and put the key back in his hand. "And I don't need another."

Daniel let out an exasperated breath. "Does everything have to be a battle between us? So I bought you a car. Sue me."

"I can't be bought."

Annoyance surged through his blood. "I'm not trying to buy you. I bought something *for* you. There's a significant difference."

"Not to me," she shot back. "First it's a car and then what…a house? Maybe one to match the house in San Francisco you want to buy? What then? A boat? What about a racehorse? Don't forget the jewels. I'll probably need a private jet, too."

"You're being ridiculous. It's just a car."

"Stop trying to justify this. Take it back. I don't want it."

He kept a lid on his simmering rage. "I want my sons to be safe, and they won't be in that jalopy," he said, and hooked a thumb in the direction of her old VW. "Be sensible, Mary-Jayne."

"I am sensible. And they'll be perfectly safe," she said hotly. "I would never put them at risk. But I won't let you tell me what to do. Not now, not ever."

He shook his head. "This isn't a multiple-choice exercise, Mary-Jayne. And I won't compromise on this issue. The car is yours." He took a few steps and dropped the key on top of the letterbox. "I want you to have it."

"I don't care what you want!"

Daniel stilled and looked at her. Her cheeks were ablaze,

her hair framing her face, her chest heaving. A thousand conflicting emotions banged around in his head. And he knew there was no reasoning with her. No middle road.

"No," he said wearily. "I guess you don't."

Then he turned around and walked down the street.

Chapter Ten

Bossy. Arrogant. Know-it-all.

Mary-Jayne had a dozen names for him and none of them were flattering.

He'd bought her a car. A car! Without discussing it with her first. Without any kind of consultation. He really did think he could do whatever he liked.

On Saturday afternoon she headed to her parents' place for lunch. The whole family got together once a month for a day of catch-up that included lunch, dinner and plenty of conversation and games with the kids. It was a Preston tradition, and since she'd missed the get-togethers while she'd been away, Mary-Jayne looked forward to spending time with them. Her father was manning the barbecue with her brother, Noah, while her brothers-in-law, Scott and Cameron, played pool in the games room, as Noah's wife, Callie, kept their kids entertained. Evie's toddler and Grace's newborn were the center of attention in the kitchen

while her mother fussed around making her famous po-
tato salad. Her best friend Lauren was there, too, with her
fiancé and her own parents. Lauren was Cameron's sister
and her fiancé, Gabe, was Scott and Callie's cousin. It was
a close-knit group. The blood ties alone made it a mam-
moth exercise to remember who was related to whom. She
cared for them all, but as she sat at the kitchen table, one
hand draped over her abdomen and the other curled around
a glass of diet soda, she experienced an inexplicable empty
feeling deep down, almost through to her bones.

She couldn't define it. She should he happy. Elated. She
had her babies growing in her belly and her whole family around her. But something was amiss. Something was
missing. *Someone was missing.*

She quickly put the idea from her head.

"Where's Daniel today?"

Her mother's cheerful voice interrupted her thoughts.
She shrugged. "I have no idea."

Barbara frowned a little. "I thought he might have liked
to come and meet everyone."

"I didn't invite him."

The room fell silent, and she looked up to see her mother's frown.

"I did," Evie added quickly. "But he said he wouldn't
come unless you asked him to be here."

Shame niggled between her shoulders. "Good. He's finally showing some sense."

Evie sighed. "What's he done now?"

Mary-Jayne couldn't miss the disapproval in her eldest sister's voice. It irritated her down to her teeth. "He
bought me a car," she said tartly. "A brand-spanking-new
BMW with all the trimmings." She laughed humorlessly.
"Imagine me driving around town in that."

The three women stared at her. It was Grace who spoke next.

"That was very thoughtful of him, don't you think? Considering how old and unreliable your current car is."

Mary-Jayne's jaw tightened. "I know it's old. And I know it's unreliable. But it's mine by choice because it's what I can afford. And he wasn't being thoughtful... He was being controlling."

Evie tutted. "Have you considered that perhaps he only wants you and the babies to be safe while you're driving?"

"That's what he said," she replied impatiently. "But I know Daniel and he—"

"Didn't his wife and baby die in a car accident?" Grace again, equally disapproving as Evie and their mother.

"Yes, they did," Evie supplied.

"And wasn't the other car involved an *old and unreliable* vehicle that had a major brake failure?"

"Yes," Evie said, looking directly at Mary-Jayne.

She sat up straight in the chair.

I don't care what you want...

Her careless words banged around in her head. Simone and their baby had died because the car that struck them had a broken brake line. She realized what he must have thought when he saw her old car—that history might repeat itself. That their sons' lives might be at risk.

It wasn't control that had motivated him to buy her a car. It was fear.

She stood up, her hands shaking. "I have to go out for a while." She looked toward Grace. "I'm parked behind you. Can you ask Cameron to move your car?"

Evie pointed to a set of keys on the counter. "Take mine," her sister suggested pointedly. "He's there alone, in case you're wondering, working in the office. My other guests left yesterday."

Mary-Jayne nodded, grabbed the keys and left.

The trip took just minutes, and she pulled the Honda Civic into the driveway. The gardens at Dunn Inn were like something out of a fairy tale, and she walked up the cobbled pathway, past the wishing well and headed up the steps to the porch. A couple of the French-style doors were open, and she slid the insect screen back. Her sister's artwork graced most walls, and the furnishings were well matched and of good quality. Evie had a style all of her own. There was a small office off the living room and when she reached the doorway she came to a halt.

Daniel sat in the chair, earphones on, tapping on the computer keys. She came behind him and touched his shoulder. He flinched and turned, tossing the earphones aside.

"Hi," she said, and dropped her tote.

He wore jeans and a blue shirt that looked as though it had been tailored to fit his gorgeous frame. His gray eyes scanned her face, his expression unreadable.

"I thought you had a family thing to go to?"

"I did," she said. "I do."

"Then, what are you doing here?"

"I left." She shrugged one shoulder. "I wanted to see you."

He swiveled the chair around and sat back. "So you're seeing me. What?"

Mary-Jayne swallowed hard. "You're working. I'm probably interrupting and—"

"What do you want, Mary-Jayne?" he asked impatiently.

She let out a long breath. "To apologize."

He stood up immediately and folded his arms. "Consider it done."

"I was wrong, okay," she said when she noticed his expression was still unmoved. "I shouldn't have reacted the way I did. I shouldn't have *overreacted*. I didn't stop to think about why it was so important to you that I have a new car." She rubbed her belly gently. "But I get it now… I understand that you need to know that our sons are safe because of what happened to your wife and daughter… You know, how the other car was old and had brake failure." Her throat thickened as she said the words. She looked at him and tried to read what he was thinking. But she couldn't. She wished she knew him better. And wished she understood the emotions behind his gray eyes.

The shutters were still up, so she pressed on.

"And I shouldn't have said that I didn't care what you wanted. I didn't mean it," she admitted.

His jaw was achingly tight. "I can't bear the thought of you driving around in that old car."

"I know," she said softly. "And I understand why you feel that way. I should have been more considerate of your feelings. But sometimes, when I'm with you, I react before I think about the consequences. It's not a conscious thing." She waved her hands. "But between you and me there's all this…tension. And getting mad at you is kind of like a release valve for that."

The mood between them suddenly altered. There *was* tension between them. Built on a blinding, blistering physical attraction that had never been truly sated. One night would never be enough for that kind of pull. Daniel had known it all along. She realized that as she stared up at him, breathing hard, chest heaving. That was why he'd pursued her for a month after Solana's birthday party. And that was why she'd refused him. She was scared of those feelings. Terrified of the way he made her feel. Because she still wanted him.

"Daniel…"

She said his name on a wispy breath. His eyes were

dark, burning and filled with desire. It was heady and commanding. It made her shake with longing and fear. Of course she wasn't afraid of him, only the hypnotic power he had over her.

He groaned, as though he knew he was about to do something he probably shouldn't. But Mary-Jayne didn't care. In that moment, with nothing between but barely a foot of space, all she wanted was to be in his arms.

"I'm trying so hard to fight this."

"I know. But it's me you're fighting," he said softly. "Not this."

He was right. She fought him. In her heart she felt she had to. But in that moment all her fight disappeared.

"Make love to me," she whispered and reached out to touch his chest.

He flinched against her touch as though it was poker hot. "Are you sure that's what you want?"

She shrugged lightly. "The only thing I'm sure about is that I'm not sure about anything anymore."

He reached for her shoulders and molded them with his hands. He fisted a handful of her hair and gently tilted her head back. "You drive me crazy, do you know that?"

She nodded a little. "I don't mean to."

"You can trust me, you know," he said and lowered his head toward her face. "I'm not your enemy. Even if it does feel as though most of the time we're at war with each other."

He kissed her then. Not gently. Not softly. But long and deep and fueled with heated possession. Mary-Jayne kissed him back and wrapped her arms around his waist. "Do you have any idea how sexy you are?" he whispered against her lips.

"No," she said, and smiled as she trailed her lips along

his jaw. "We've got the place to ourselves… Let's not waste any time."

He got her to his room in ten seconds flat. He closed the door and locked it.

They stood opposite one another by the bed. Last time there'd been no thinking, nothing but desire and pure instinct. This was different. This was conscious and planned and fueled by more than simple attraction.

"Do you know what I thought the first time I saw you?" he asked quietly.

Mary-Jayne shook her head.

"I thought," he said as he reached for her, "that I had never seen a woman with such beautiful hair in all my life."

He kissed her again, and she shuddered and tossed her head. When he pulled back she was breathing so hard she thought her lungs might explode. He slipped her T-shirt off one shoulder and trailed his mouth along her collarbone. There was such blistering intensity in his touch that it thrilled her to the soles of her feet. He kept kissing her, making her sigh and moan until finally she begged him to take her to the bed.

"What's the hurry?" he muttered against her neck.

Mary-Jayne ran her hands over his chest. His heart beat furiously behind his ribs and her hand hovered there for a moment. Last time they'd made love as if there was no time to waste. But now he seemed in no rush to get her naked and between the sheets. He was taking his time exploring her mouth with his own and gently smoothing his hands across her back and shoulders. They stood kissing like that for minutes. Or was it hours? She couldn't tell. She was too overwhelmed by the narcotic pleasure thrumming through her body at the seductive tone of his skilled touch. By the time they worked their way to the side of the bed she was a wriggling mass of need.

He stripped the T-shirt over her head and Mary-Jayne watched, fascinated as he slowly undressed her. It was intensely erotic and made her long for him with such urgency she could barely breathe. When she was naked, when her shirt was on the floor and her bra dispensed with, he hooked his thumbs under the band of her briefs and slowly skimmed them down over her bottom and legs. Then he was on his knees in front of her, touching her belly, pressing kisses across the curved, tightened skin. She'd never experienced anything more intimate or soul reaching in her entire life. He reached up to cup her breasts, and they felt heavy in his hands. As he gently toyed with her nipples, every part of her body felt more alive, more sensitive to his touch than ever before.

She whispered his name, and he looked up to meet her gaze. He was still fully dressed and she wanted nothing more than to feel his skin against her, to wrap herself in his embrace and feel his body deep within hers. Mary-Jayne curled her fingers around his shirt collar and found the top button. She flicked it open with eager hands.

"Take this off," she instructed with way more bravado than she felt.

He smiled, urged her to sit, and once she was settled on the bed he shrugged out of his shirt. Shoes and socks and jeans followed, and once he was naked he sat beside her.

"Better?" he asked, reaching for her again, kissing her neck and shoulders.

Mary-Jayne sighed heavily. "Much."

He palmed her rounded belly. "Pregnancy has made you even more beautiful, if that were possible."

It was a lovely thought. She'd never considered herself all that beautiful. Not like her sister Grace. Or Evie, with her dancing eyes and seductive curves. She was pretty at best. Not even particularly sexy. But beneath Daniel's glittering gaze she felt more beautiful than she ever had in her life.

She placed a hand on her belly. "Are we going to be able to do this?" she asked, smiling a little. "My middle is expanding at an alarming rate."

Daniel grasped her hand and spanned his own across her stomach. "I'm sure we'll manage just fine, darling."

Darling...

It was the first endearment he'd said to her. And it sounded so lovely coming from his lips that emotion unexpectedly gathered at the back of her eyes. She wanted that and more. Despite every argument and every rational part of her brain telling her it was madness—she wanted to be the woman he called darling every day of his life.

Because...

Because she loved him.

She'd fallen in love with the father of her babies. Wholly and completely. Even knowing that he didn't love her back and that he was all wrong for her and she for him. None of that mattered. Her heart had decided.

"What are you thinking?" he asked.

Mary-Jayne shook her head. "Nothing... Just...kiss me."

He smiled and found her mouth again. His kiss was long and slow and everything she wanted. She kissed him back with every ounce of feeling in her heart. He lowered her onto the bed and began to make love to her with such excruciating sweetness she could barely stop herself from calling out his name. He touched her, stroked her and worshipped her breasts with his mouth and hands until she was quivering in his arms. By the time he moved his hand between her legs to caress her she was so fueled with passion she rose up and over and found release almost immediately. It was wondrously intense, and when she came back to earth and the stars had stopped exploding behind her eyes she saw that he was staring down into her face.

"What's wrong?" she asked tremulously, pushing air into her lungs.

"Not a thing," he replied, and kissed her again. "So I guess we don't have to be too concerned about birth control?"

She grinned and stretched. "The horse has already bolted on that one."

Daniel laughed and rolled over, positioning himself between her legs. She relaxed her thighs and waited, so consumed with love for him in that moment that if he'd asked her for the moon she would had flown into the sky to catch it for him.

When they were together, when she couldn't tell when she began and he ended, Mary-Jayne let out a contented moan. He moved against her with such acute tenderness her heart literally ached. Nothing had ever felt so good. And she'd never been more connected to anyone than she was with him as he hovered above her, taking most of his weight on his strong arms, ensuring she was comfortable and relaxed. Release came to her again, slow and languorous and fulfilling, and when he shuddered above her she held on, gripping him tighter, longer and with more feeling than she ever had before in her life.

When he moved and rolled over onto his back, they were both breathing madly. Mary-Jayne closed her eyes and sighed. When her breathing returned with some normalcy she shifted onto her side and looked at him. His chest rose and fell, and he had his eyes closed. He reached for her hand and linked their fingers.

"You know," he said, and sighed, "we should do it down on the beach."

"Do what?" she asked, and kissed his shoulder. "This?"

"Get married. What else?"

Mary-Jayne stilled. A little voice at the back of her mind chanted that she should grab his idea with both hands and say a resounding *yes*. But she couldn't. He didn't love her. He never would. Sure, the sex was incredible and she had his babies growing inside her, but not even that was enough to sustain a lifetime relationship. He had to know that. Only a fool would believe otherwise. She loved him. But she wasn't about to become strapped to a one-side marriage.

"You said you wouldn't ask again," she reminded him.

He shrugged. "I can't help it. I want what I want."

"I can't."

"Or won't?" he asked.

"Both," she admitted, and rolled onto her back. "Can't we just get to know one another a little, Daniel? I mean, I hardly know anything about you and—"

"Because you've never asked," he said a little more harshly. "Okay—I'm thirty-four and recently had a birthday. My favorite color is yellow and I loathe brussels sprouts. When I was fifteen I chipped my two front teeth and now I have veneers. I was seventeen the first time I had sex and since my wife died I've slept with just over half a dozen women. I like imported beer but rarely drink. I haven't had a meaningful conversation with my dad in years and I still think it sucks that I never knew my real mom." He pulled himself up and draped the sheet across his hips. "Satisfied?"

Mary-Jayne sat up and covered her bare breasts with her arms. "That's not what I meant. I'm talking about time. We need time to get to know one another."

"We don't have it," he said flatly. "You live here. I live in San Francisco. I need an answer, Mary-Jayne."

She pulled herself across the bed and got to her feet. "Then, it's no."

* * *

No. Again.

Was there a bigger sucker than him?

Daniel sprang out of the bed and watched her as she snatched up her clothes. "You're being rash...as usual."

"I'm being honest," she said, and pulled on her underwear. "And sure, I'm impulsive and over the years it has gotten me into trouble every now and then. But in this I'm not being rash. I'm using my head," she said, and looked him over with deliberate emphasis. "And not the part of my anatomy that you are if you think having great sex is enough of a reason to get married."

"They're the reason," he said, and pulled on his jeans as he motioned to her belly. "Our children. The great sex is a bonus."

She tossed a shoe at him. And then another.

The first one hit him in the shoulder and the second sandal he caught midair. There was so much fire and spirit in her, so much passion. Daniel was inexplicably drawn to her like a moth to a flame. He liked that she wasn't a pushover, even though it drove him to distraction. "Stop throwing things at me."

"Well, you stop doing what you're doing and I will."

Daniel dropped the shoe and shrugged, holding out his hands. "What have I done now?"

"You know exactly what," she said on a rush of breath. "You know how I feel, Daniel. I don't want to get married and live somewhere else. I want to live here, in Crystal Point. I want our children to grow up in a home, not a house. And I want my family around me while I raise them."

"While *you* raise them?" he said flatly. "Which is exactly my point. *We* need to raise them, Mary-Jayne, together. And I think today proved that we can. We have a connection that's—"

"We had sex," she corrected. "But it's not enough. The truth is, you confuse me when you kiss me and touch me, and then I can't get any of this straight in my mind. I won't let you use sex as a way of—"

"*You* came here today, remember?" he reminded her, cutting her off. "*You* asked me to make love to *you*, remember? Not the other way around. I've left you alone these past few days…just as you asked."

She stilled. "But…"

Her words trailed and she glared at him, her eyes glittering with a kind of fiery rage. She was brash and argumentative and generally on the attack…but caught out, and she was as meek as a lamb. She was a fascinating contradiction. And he craved her more than he'd ever wanted any woman in his life.

"You came here today looking for me. For this," he said and gestured to the bed. "Because we have an insane attraction for one another that neither of us expected."

She sucked in a long breath. "I came here today because I felt bad for what I said the other day. I felt guilty, okay?"

"So today was about sympathy? Throw a crumb to the lonely widower whose wife and baby died?"

"No," she said quickly. "Of course not. I just thought we could…talk, that's all."

"Talk about what?" he asked. "You and me? There is no you and me, right? Or do you want to know about Simone? Or our daughter? What do you want to know? How long I sat in hospital the night my wife died? Eight hours," he said, feeling the memory of those hours through to the marrow in his bones. "Do you also want to know that I never got to say goodbye to her? I never got a chance to tell her what she meant to me—hell, I never even said it enough when she was alive. And yes, I held my daughter's lifeless body for a few moments before they took her away. Do you want to know if I cried? Once, after the wake when everyone had left and I realized for the rest of my life I'd be living with the fact that my daughter's birthday was the same day she and her mom died."

He stopped speaking and looked at Mary-Jayne. Her eyes brimmed with tears, and he immediately felt bad. He didn't want to upset her. He wanted to do the exact opposite, if she'd only let him.

"I'm so sorry…"

"You can't have it both ways," he said as he retrieved her skirt and T-shirt and passed them to her. "Yes, my wife and baby died. And yes, sometimes I feel alone *and* lonely because of that. Who the hell doesn't feel alone at times? But if you want to be here, then really be here, Mary-Jayne. Stop making excuses."

"I'm not," she said, wiping her eyes before she quickly slipped into her clothes.

"You are," he said, suddenly impatient. "And the next time you turn up on my door and ask me to make love to you, it'll only happen if my ring is on your finger."

"Then it will never happen again."

He shrugged, pretty sure she didn't believe that any more than he did. "You should get back to your party."

She shoved her feet into her shoes. "Would you like to come with me?"

He cocked one brow. "Are you sure that's what you want?"

"What I want is for us to get along for the sake of our children." She planted her hands on her hips and spoke in a quiet voice. "I'm trying to be rational and realistic. I don't want to be trapped in a loveless and empty marriage. And if you're honest with yourself, if you can think of only that and not about custody of the babies or how challenging it's going to be to raise them together when we live on opposite sides of the world, you'd realize that you don't want that, either. Especially after the way you loved your wife."

A loveless and empty marriage? Was that what she truly thought it would be? Were her feelings for him that hollow? He did his best to ignore the way that idea made him feel.

"I want," he said with deliberate emphasis, "my family."

"So do I," she said quietly. "But *my* family is here, Daniel. In Crystal Point. I like living a few streets away from my parents and having my sisters and brother close by. I don't come from a family where we greet one another with a handshake and live in different parts of the world. I like knowing that 'I love you' is the last thing I hear from my mother when I hang up the phone after I speak to her, and I like knowing that my dad would be there for me in a heartbeat if I needed him. And maybe that sounds like a silly TV movie to you, but it's what I want for my children."

For a second he envied her. It didn't sound silly at all. It sounded real and authentic and exactly what he'd hoped he'd have for his own children one day. Being around Mary-Jayne and her family had only amplified that need. He wanted to tell her that. But he held back.

I don't want to be trapped in a loveless and empty marriage.

That was what she imagined they'd have. Not a marriage like her siblings' or her parents'. But something less, something that would never measure up to the standards she witnessed in her life. It would never be enough. They would never be enough.

"We should get going," he said, and grabbed his shirt. "I would like to see your parents again."

She nodded and made her way across the room.

They drove separate cars to her parents' home. Him in his rental. She in her sister's Honda. He knew the BMW still sat outside her house. She hadn't driven it once, he was sure. She was stubborn and infuriating. When they arrived at the Preston house, he got out and met her by her car door, not saying a word about the old VW he spotted in the driveway, even though he hated the idea of her driving something so unreliable and potentially dangerous.

"I'm sorry about before," he said, and took her elbow. "I didn't mean to make you cry."

She sniffed. "Okay...sure."

He rubbed her skin. "I don't enjoy seeing you upset."

She nodded, eyes still glistening. "I know that. I don't mean to upset you, either. I just don't seem to be able to help myself sometimes."

Inside, he was welcomed by her family with the warmth he'd come to expect from them. They were good people, and it made him think about the dig she'd made about handshakes and living on opposite sides of the world. She was right. He was close to his brothers but not in the way she was with her siblings. And his relationship with Miles and Bernadette had been taxing most of his life.

He was by the pool talking to her brother and enduring a moderate kind of grilling about his intentions when his phone rang. He excused himself and picked up the call on the fifth ring.

It was Caleb.

Daniel listened to his brother's concerned voice, and once he ended the call went looking for Mary-Jayne. She was inside, in the kitchen with her mother and sister-in-law.

"I need to talk to you," he said, and ignored the thunder behind his ribs.

She must have picked up on his mood, because she

complied immediately and ushered him into the front living room.

"What is it?" she asked once they were alone.

"I have to leave."

"Oh, okay. I'll see you Monday, then. Remember I have an appointment with my OB at ten."

"I'm leaving Crystal Point," he said again, firmer. "Caleb just called me—Bernie's in the hospital in Cairns. She had a massive heart attack a couple of hours ago."

Mary-Jayne gasped and gripped his arm. "Oh, how awful. Is there anything I can do?"

Marry me and stay by my side…

He reached out and touched her belly, felt the movement of his babies beneath his palm and experienced such an acute sensation in his chest he could barely breathe. The connection was mesmerizing. Her green eyes glittered brilliantly, and he got so caught up in her gaze he was rooted to the spot.

"I could… I could…" Her voice trailed off.

"What?" he asked.

She shrugged a little. "I'm not sure… I just thought perhaps I could…"

She could what? Come with him? A part of him wanted that more than anything. But that couldn't be what she meant. She'd have to care one way or another. Daniel swallowed hard. "Take care of yourself, Mary-Jayne."

"You, too," she whispered. "Give your dad and Bernie my love."

But not you…

He got the message loud and clear.

"I'll talk to you soon."

"Please let me know how she is."

Daniel nodded, suddenly numb all over. "Sure." He

shrugged off her touch and walked to the door, but something stopped him. Then he turned and looked at her.

"What?" she asked softly.

"I've just realized that you're a fraud, Mary-Jayne," he said. "You walk and talk like some restless free spirit who can take on the world, but underneath all that talk is someone who's afraid to truly be who she is."

She frowned. "That doesn't make sense."

"Doesn't it? You've wrapped yourself up in this image of being a certain kind of person and it's as though you've locked yourself in a cage. Admit it, if I was some unemployed, tattooed and unsuccessful guitarist things would be very different. You'd have nothing to hide behind. You say you don't want to be trapped in a loveless marriage— but that's not it. You just don't want to marry *me*. Because if you did it would mean that everything you've ever stood for is a great big lie. It would mean that you've settled for the safe road, and then everyone around you would know that your boldness and bluster is just an act and that you're as mainstream and sensible as the rest of us. And that's what scares you—being like everyone else. That's why your last boyfriend was a deadbeat and why your business fails to get off the ground. You think that makes you a free spirit? You're wrong… All that makes you is a coward."

Then he turned on his heel and left.

Chapter Eleven

"Are you still feeling unwell?" Evie's voice cut through her thoughts.

Mary-Jayne battened down the nausea she'd been battling for a week. She'd spent the morning babysitting her niece while Evie and Scott attended an art show in Bellandale. She loved looking after Rebecca and considered it good practice for when her babies arrived.

"On and off. The crackers help a little, but yesterday I spent an hour bent over the toilet bowl. I saw my doctor the other day and we discussed some medication I can take to alleviate the nausea if it gets much worse. I just don't want to do anything that might harm my babies. But after yesterday I think I'm going to have to take his advice. I've got another doctor's appointment tomorrow at three."

Evie grimaced. "That's not much fun. Other than that, is everything going okay?"

"With the pregnancy? Yes, no problems. Except I'm getting as big as a house."

"You look lovely as always," Evie assured her. "Heard from Daniel?"

"Nope."

Evie's brows furrowed. "Everything okay on that front?"

"Nope," she said and sighed. "We sort of had a fight before he left."

"Just a fight? Anything else?"

Her sister was way too intuitive. Mary-Jayne shrugged. She wasn't about to admit he'd called her a coward, or that it was exactly how she felt. "Sex isn't enough to sustain a marriage…no matter how good it is."

Evie came around the kitchen counter and rested her hands on the back of a dining chair. "Why didn't you go with him?"

She shrugged, hurting all over. "He didn't ask me."

"Maybe he thought you'd say no."

She shrugged again, still hurting, and more confused than ever. She wasn't about to admit to her sister that she missed him like crazy. "I'm not part of his life in that way."

"But you're lovers?"

Heat crept over her skin. She could never lie to Evie. "I guess. Does one night and one afternoon together make us lovers? I'm not sure what that makes us. All it makes me is confused."

"But you're in love with him, right?"

"It doesn't matter what I am," she insisted. "I can love him until the cows come home and it won't change the fact that he doesn't love me back."

"Are you sure?"

"Positive," she replied, aching deep down. She pressed her hands to her belly and rubbed her babies as they moved inside her. "He's all one-eyed about what he thinks we should do. Which is get married and raise our children in San Francisco."

"He said that?" she asked. "He said he wants you to move there?"

She nodded. "Well, he offered to buy me a house so I can live there for six months of the year."

Evie tilted her head. "I thought he might have decided he liked it here."

Mary-Jayne's eyes popped wide. "Daniel live here? In Crystal Point?" She laughed shrilly. "Not likely. Too hometown for him. He's all business and logic. He'd be bored out of his mind in a place like this."

Her sister smiled. "Really? He looked pretty comfortable here to me. And since when did you get all stuck on Crystal Point as a be-all and end-all? You spent a good part of the past ten years away from here, traveling from one place to the next." Her brows came back up. "I can remember a certain nineteen-year-old telling me in no uncertain terms that it was the most boring, uneventful spot on the map before you hopped on a plane for Morocco. I think the folks thought you'd closed your eyes and pointed to a spot on an atlas and thought, 'Why not go there?' And then there was Thailand, and Cambodia, and after that it was Mexico. And wasn't it you who spent three months backpacking through Greece and working transient jobs and peddling your jewelry to patrons in sidewalk cafés to make ends meet? And didn't you recently leave here to bail out your old school friend in Port Douglas with only a day's notice?" Evie smiled. "What's happened, M.J.? Have you lost your restless spirit? Have you realized that this little town is not such a bad place after all?"

"I never thought it was bad. I love this town. I've just

always loved traveling and experiencing new places, that's all."

"New places except San Francisco?"

Mary-Jayne stilled. Evie had a point. "You think I should do it? You think I should marry him and move to another country?"

"I think you should do whatever your heart tells you is right."

"That's what I'm doing," she insisted.

"Your heart," Evie said pointedly. "Not your head."

But my heart will get pummeled, for sure...

"I can't." She stood and grabbed her bag. "I have to get going."

Her sister nodded. "Okay. Thank you for babysitting. Rebecca loves spending time with you."

Mary-Jayne smiled broadly. "It's mutual."

Evie reached out and hugged her tight. "By the way, I see you're driving the Beamer."

Mary-Jayne wondered how long it would take for her sister to remark about the car parked along the front curb. She shrugged. "Seemed silly to let it sit there, that's all."

"Smart move. Is it good to drive?"

"Like a dream," she admitted, and grinned. "And two baby seats arrived for it yesterday."

Evie's smiled widened. "He thought of everything, didn't he?"

"Pretty much," she replied, ignoring the jab of pain in her chest. "Anyway, I have to run."

"Let me know how things go at the doctor's."

"Will do," she said as she left.

By the time she got home it was after four. She fed the dog and parrot and took a shower and then changed into baggy sweats and flaked out on the sofa. She flicked channels on the television and stared absently at the screen for an hour. Later, she ate a grilled-cheese sandwich and attempted to do some work on a new bracelet for one of Solana's friends. But she couldn't concentrate. Her mind was filled with thoughts of Daniel and his parting words.

Four days after Daniel left, Mary-Jayne got a text from Audrey informing her that Bernie was finally off the critical list but still in intensive care. There was no word from Daniel. It had been a long, lonely week. Part of her was glad. Part of her never wanted to see him again. Another part missed him so much she ached inside.

Coward...

The word had resonated in her head for days. No one had ever called her that before. No one would ever dare. But not Daniel. He called it how it was. He made her accountable for her convictions. For the first time in her life Mary-Jayne felt as though she had met her match. Her *perfect* match.

If only he loved her...

But he didn't. He thought that physical attraction was enough to sustain a marriage. But in her heart she knew it wasn't. He was kidding himself. Sure, maybe for the first few years everything would be okay. They'd be busy raising their children and there wouldn't be time to think about how loveless their marriage was. But later, once the children were older and there was only them, their differences would be evident and insurmountable. It was an impossible situation. And she wouldn't do it. She couldn't. She owed her babies more than a life where their parents were together for the wrong reasons.

As much as she appreciated her sister's support, Evie didn't really understand. She'd fallen madly in love with Scott and he'd loved her in return. He'd wooed her and fought for her and laid his heart on the line as if nothing else mattered. But Daniel... There was no heart in his proposal. Only logic and his desire to share custody of their sons.

And that would never be enough.

Five days after arriving back in Port Douglas, Daniel and his brothers were still maintaining a rotating vigil outside Bernie's hospital room. Their father hadn't left his wife's side, and at seven o'clock on Thursday evening, Daniel headed for the small hospital cafeteria and returned with two double-shot espressos. Bernie had finally been taken off the critical list, and Blake and Caleb had gone back to the resort to get some much-needed rest while Daniel stayed with his father, ensuring Miles at least ate and drank something.

"Here," he said, and passed his father a take-out cup as he sat in one of the uncomfortable chairs outside the intensive care ward. "And don't let it get cold like the last one I gave you."

Miles managed a grin and then nodded. "Thanks."

His father's pain was palpable. "She's out of danger, Dad. That's good news."

"I know," Miles said, and sighed. "I don't think I could have taken another night of wondering if she was going to make it."

"You heard what the doctor said a few hours ago," he assured his father. "She's going to pull through and be back to her old self in no time."

His dad sighed again. "Who would have thought this might happen? I mean, she's always been so health conscious... I never would have guessed she had a weak heart."

"No one can predict the future, Dad."

His words felt hollow as they left his mouth. How often had he thought that? When his grandfather passed away?

When Simone and their baby died? When Mary-Jayne told him she was pregnant?

"Yeah, I know," his dad said, and tapped him on the shoulder. "Thanks for being here this week. It's meant a lot to me."

"I wouldn't be anywhere else."

Miles shrugged a little. "I know you've got a lot going on."

Daniel drank some coffee and stared at the wall ahead.

"You should go back," Miles said quietly. "You need to sort it out."

"Actually, I think a little time apart might be what we both need."

He wasn't about to admit that he missed Mary-Jayne more than he'd believed possible. But he hadn't called her, even though he craved the sound of her voice. And he was right about thinking they needed some time out.

"Nonsense," his dad said gently. "Time apart serves no purpose. Because one day you might find you have no time left, right?"

Daniel looked at his father. Miles had one of his serious expressions on his face, and as much as Daniel wanted to fob the other man off, he resisted. He'd seen that look once before, right after his grandfather had died and Daniel was preparing to step into the role of CEO. Miles had tried to talk him out of it. At the time, Daniel was convinced his father lacked vision and ambition and simply wanted to sell the company. And it had taken years for that idea to fade. It wasn't until the wake after Simone's death that he'd realized that there was more to life than business. More to life than seventy-hour weeks and meetings and racing to catch flights from one corner of the globe to the other. But still, he hadn't changed. He'd kept on doing the same things. He'd drowned himself in work to avoid thinking about all he'd lost.

"How about we concentrate on Bernie getting better and—"

"I'm very proud of you, you know," Miles said, uncharacteristically cutting him off. "I'm very proud of the man you have become."

Daniel's throat thickened. "Dad, I—"

"And I know I never say it enough." His father shrugged. "I guess I'm not sure if that matters to you."

"It matters," he said quietly. "The talking thing… It goes both ways."

Miles smiled. "Your mom was always telling me I needed to talk more to my own father. When you were born I promised myself I'd be a better father than Mike Anderson…but I'm not sure I have been. When your mom died I fell apart. Thankfully Bernie came along and picked up the pieces, even though she had every reason to run a mile. I was a grieving man with a baby, and I had so much emotional baggage it's a wonder she was able to see through all that and still give me a shot."

"She loved you," Daniel said, and drank some coffee.

"Not at first, she didn't," Miles said. "Some days I think she might have hated me. But we worked it out." His father nodded and grinned a little. "And you will, too."

Daniel didn't share his dad's optimism. Mary-Jayne opposed him at every opportunity. And he couldn't see a way out of it. He wanted her, sure. And sometimes…sometimes it felt as though he needed her like he needed air in his lungs. But it wasn't anything more than that. How could it be? They hardly knew one another. She was dreaming about some silly romantic notion that simply didn't exist. So maybe he did think about her 24/7. And maybe he did long for her in ways he'd never longed for anyone before.

But that was just desire and attraction. Add in the fact that he wanted the chance to be a full-time father to his sons…and of course it might seem like something else. Something more.

"I loved your mom," Miles said quietly. "But I love Bernie, too. It's not more, it's not less… It's simply a different kind of same."

A different kind of same…

He was still thinking about his father's words for hours afterward. And still when he tried to sleep later that night. His dreams were plagued by images of Mary-Jayne. He dreamed of holding her, of making love to her, of waking up with her hair fanned out on the pillow beside him. He awoke restless and missing her more than he'd imagined he could. And in the cold light of morning he realized one irrefutable fact.

He was in love with her.

And their relationship had just become a whole lot more complicated.

On Monday, with the nausea and lack of appetite still lingering, she went back to her doctor to discuss some medication and get her blood pressure checked. She was waiting for the doctor to come into the room when Julie, an old school friend and now the receptionist from the front desk, popped her head around the door.

"M.J.," she said and made a face. "There's someone out here who wants to see you. Who *insists* on seeing you."

She perched herself on the edge of the chair. "Who?"

Julie's eyes widened dramatically. "He says he's your fiancé."

The blood left her face. There could only be one possibility. "Oh…okay," she said, trying not to have a reaction that Julie would see through and then question. "Tall, dark hair, handsome, gray eyes?"

Julie nodded. "Oh, yeah, that's him."

She managed a smile. "You should probably send him through."

"Okay, sure."

She disappeared, and barely seconds later the door opened and Daniel strode into the room. Mary-Jayne looked him over. He seemed so familiar and yet like such a stranger. He wore dark chinos and a creaseless pale blue shirt. Her heart skipped a beat. She'd never found any man as attractive as him. And doubted she ever would. And deep down, in that place she'd come to harbor all her feelings for him, she was happy to see him. More than happy. Right then, in that moment, she didn't feel alone.

She took a breath and met his gaze. "Fiancé?"

He shrugged loosely. "Got me in the room, didn't it?"

She didn't flinch. "What are you doing here? How did you—"

"Your sister told me I'd find you here."

She nodded. "So you're back?"

"I'm back." He moved across the room and sat beside her.

"How's your mother?"

He rested back in the seat a little. "Out of intensive care. She had major bypass surgery for two blocked arteries. She's doing okay now. She'll be in the hospital for another week, though. So why are you here? Checkup?"

Mary-Jayne tried to ignore how her insides fluttered from being so close to him. "I haven't been feeling well and—"

"You're sick?" he asked and jackknifed up straight. "What's wrong? Is it the babies?" he asked and reached out to touch her abdomen.

She flinched a little from his touch, and he noticed im
mediately because he snatched his hand away. "Just nau
sea again. And I've lost my appetite."

He frowned. "Why didn't you call me? I would have
come back sooner."

She pressed her shoulders back. "You needed to be with
your family. It was important for your parents."

"I need to be here for you," he said with emphasis.
"That's important, too."

"I'm fine," she insisted, feeling like a fool for thinking
his concern must mean he cared. Well, of course he cared.
She was carrying his babies. But caring wasn't love. And
love was all she'd accept.

He inspected her face with his smoky gaze. "You look
pale."

"Stop fussing," she said and frowned. "I'm fine, like
said. Just tired and not all that hungry because of the nau
sea. But I'm sure it will pass soon."

The doctor entered then, and she was glad for the re
prieve. Until Daniel started barking out questions about
her fatigue, her blood pressure and the likelihood of risks
associated with the antinausea medication the doctor sug
gested she take if the symptoms didn't abate soon. She
gave Daniel a death stare—which he ignored completely.

The doctor, a mild-mannered man in his fifties, just
nodded and answered the questions in a patient voice.
When he said he was going to draw some blood, Daniel
almost rocketed out of his seat.

"Why? What's wrong?" he asked. "If you think there's
a risk to her health then I insist we—"

"It's okay," she assured him and grasped his arm. "It's
just a blood test. Remember how I told you that my sister
had gestational diabetes? It's only precautionary."

She thought he might pass out when the nurse came

in and took the blood. To his credit he sat in the chair and watched the entire thing, unflinching. When it was over and the doctor passed her a note with some more vitamins he wanted her to take, Daniel got to his feet and wobbled a little. She grabbed his hand and held on. Once they were in the corridor she slowed down and looked up at him, smiling.

"My hero."

He frowned. "It's not funny."

"Sure it is. Big, strong fella like you afraid of a little old needle... Who would have thought it possible?"

"I'm not afraid of them," he said, and grasped her fingers, entwining them with his own until their palms were flat against each other. "I simply don't like them. And just because you aren't afraid of anything, Mary-Jayne, doesn't mean you should make fun of people who are."

She grinned, despite the fact she was shaking inside. Holding his hand, making jokes and simply *being* with him shouldn't have made her so happy. But it did. Even though in her heart she knew it wasn't real. When they were outside he looked around.

"Where's your car?"

She took a second and then pointed to the BMW parked a few spots from the entrance. "Over there."

He glanced at the car and then to her. "Good to see you're coming to your senses."

She shrugged. "I hate waste, that's all. The car seats arrived, too... That was very thoughtful of you."

He gave her a wry smile. "Oh, you know me, an arrogant, entitled jerk and all that."

Mary-Jayne blew out a flustered breath. "Okay...so you're not all bad."

"Not all bad?" he echoed. "That's quite a compliment."

"All right, I'm an ungrateful coward who has been determined to see the worst in you from the moment we met. Satisfied?"

He smiled. "I shouldn't have called you that. I was frustrated and annoyed and worried about my mom and took it out on you. I missed you, by the way, in case you were wondering."

She nodded as emotion tightened her throat. "I might have missed you a little, too."

"I should have taken you with me."

She ached to tell him that was what she'd hoped for. But she didn't say it. "Well, I'm glad she's going to get well."

"Me, too," he said, and grinned. "So, truce?"

She smiled back at him. "I guess. Where are you staying this time? The B and B?"

He shrugged. "I'm not sure. I didn't get the chance to talk to your sister about it. Once she told me where you were I bailed and headed here."

"Would you like to stay for dinner tonight?" she asked.

He nodded. "I would. But I'll cook."

She gave him a colorful glare. "Are you suggesting that my cooking is below par?"

"I'm saying your cooking is woeful." He grabbed her hand and squeezed her fingers gently. "I'll stop at the supermarket and get what we need, and then I'll see you at home."

Home...

It sounded so nice the way he said it. The fluttering she'd had in her belly since he'd first walked into the doctor's office increased tenfold. "Okay, see you a little later."

And then he kissed her. Softly, sweetly. Like a man kissed a woman he cared about. Mary-Jayne's leaping heart almost came through her chest. And if she'd had any doubts that she'd fallen in love with him, they quickly disappeared.

* * *

Daniel pulled up outside Mary-Jayne's house a little over an hour later. He'd been all wound up in knots earlier in the morning at the thought of seeing her again, but the moment he'd opened the door and spotted her in the chair in her doctor's office, hands clasped together and her beautiful hair framing her face, all the anxiety had disappeared. She hadn't looked unhappy to see him. She'd looked…relieved. As if she welcomed him there. As if she wanted him there. Which was more than he deserved after the insensitive words he'd left her with, right before he'd returned to Port Douglas to be with his family.

He'd had a lot of time to think about their relationship in the past week. Sitting in the hospital waiting room with his father had been incredibly humbling and at times fraught with emotion. Memories of his own wife had bombarded him. Of the night they'd brought Simone into emergency and he'd arrived too late. She was already unconscious. Already too far gone for the doctors to try to save her. And then he'd waited while they'd delivered their baby and hoped that a miracle would happen and their daughter would survive. But she hadn't, and he'd lost them both.

And while he'd waited at the hospital after Bernie's surgery he'd really talked to his dad for the first time since forever. About Bernie, about his own mother, about Simone and their baby. And about Mary-Jayne. Miles had been strong, more resilient than he'd imagined. He'd wanted to comfort his dad, and in the end it happened the other way around. He was ashamed to remember how he'd always considered his father as weak. As a kind man, but one driven by his emotions. Daniel had mistaken Miles's lack of ambition as a failing. But he was wrong. His father's ambitions were simply different from his own. And yet, in some ways, very much the same. Because Miles had endeavored to be a worthy, caring dad to his sons, and Daniel was determined to emulate that ambition. He wanted to be around his sons and watch them grow into children and then teens and finally into adulthood. He wanted to share their lives and be the best man he could be for them. And for Mary-Jayne, too. He cared about her too much to simply let her be only the mother of his sons. He wanted more. He *needed* more.

And since he'd screwed up big time in the courtship department, he had to go back to square one and start all over again. Like he should have done in the beginning, on that first time they'd met. Instead of making that stupid, off-the-cuff comment about how they'd end up in his condo at some point, he should have asked her out. He should have wooed her and courted her like she deserved. He should have gone to see her while she was in South Dakota at her friend's wedding and pursued her properly, and not asked her to meet him on his turf as though all he was interested in was getting her into bed. No wonder she'd turned him down flat. And since then they'd been at war—arguing and insulting one another. She'd called him arrogant and she was right. He'd come out fighting on every occasion and hadn't let her really get to know him at all.

She wants romance and all the trimmings...

Well, he could do that if it meant she would eventually agree to marry him.

He walked up the path and saw that her old car had a for-sale sign propped inside the back window. It pleased him, and by the time he reached her door he was grinning like a fool.

"Oh, hi," she said, breathless and beautiful in a white floaty dress that came to her knees and buttoned down the front. Her belly had popped out more and she looked so beautiful he couldn't do anything other than stare at her. "Come inside."

He crossed the threshold and walked down the hall. Her little dog came yapping around his ankles, and he made a point of patting the animal for a moment before he entered the kitchen.

"So what are you making?" she asked when he put the bags on the counter.

He started unpacking the bags. "Vegetarian tagine… Spiced carrots…amongst other things."

Her green eyes widened. "Moroccan?" She laughed and the sound rushed over his skin and through his blood. "My favorite."

"Want to help?"

She nodded and tossed an apron at him. "Only if you wear this."

He opened up the garment and read the words *Kiss The Cook*. "Really?"

She shrugged. "You never know your luck."

He popped it over his head. "I already feel lucky."

She came around the counter and methodically tied it round the back. "You mean because of your mother? You must be so relieved that she's out of danger."

"We all are," he said, thinking how he was imagining he'd get to kiss her again and that was why he felt lucky. "My dad couldn't bear to lose her."

"I can imagine," she said, and pulled a couple of cutting boards from a drawer. "I mean, he already lost your mother, so to lose Bernie, too… I mean, I know your mother was the love of his life because Solana told me… but he loves Bernie dearly, you can tell by the way he looks at her."

Daniel stopped what he was doing and stared at her. Her green eyes shimmered so brilliantly it was impossible to

look anywhere else. The awareness between them amplified tenfold, and he fought the urge to reach for her and
take her in his arms. Instead he met her gaze and spoke
"Just because he loved my mom didn't mean he had less
of himself to give to someone else."

She inhaled sharply. "I...I suppose so... I mean, if he
was willing to open his heart."

"He was," Daniel said quietly. "He did."

The meaning was not lost on either of them. "And
they've had a good marriage, Mary-Jayne. They got married quickly and didn't really know one another very well
But it worked. It *can* work."

She started to nod and then stopped. "But they love
one another."

"They do now. They got married, had children
made a life together. So perhaps it did start out a little
unorthodox...but in the end it's how it plays out that's important."

She didn't look completely convinced and as much as
he wanted to keep pushing, he backed off and returned his
attention to the grocery bags on the counter. They chatted
about mundane things, like her new car and the weather
She asked after his grandmother and was clearly delighted
when he told her Solana wanted to come to Crystal Point
for a visit.

"She'd like it here," he said when the food was cooking. He stood by the stove, stirring the pot. "Once Bernie
is assured of a full recovery, I'm sure my grandmother
will come."

"I'd like that," she said as she grabbed plates and cutlery and took them to the table. "Um...how long are you
staying for this time?"

He kept stirring. "I'm not sure. I have to get back to

work at some point. I need to go to Phuket for the reopening once the renovation is complete in a couple of weeks."

She nodded, eyed the salad he'd made and sniffed the air appreciatively. "That smells good. You really do know how to cook."

He grinned. "Told you," he said, and then more seriously, "There's a lot you don't know about me, Mary-Jayne. But I'd like to change that. You said we should take some time and you were right. But I don't want to pressure you. So if you want slow, then we'll go slow."

She stopped what she was doing and looked at him. "Honestly, I don't know what I want."

"How about you take some time to figure it out?"

"You said we didn't have time."

He shrugged loosely. "I was mad at you when I said that. We have time."

She nodded a little and took a couple of sodas out of the fridge. "I don't have any of that imported beer you like," she said, and placed the cans on the counter. "But I can get some."

"This is fine," he said, and cranked both lids. "I don't drink much."

They ate a leisurely dinner and she entertained him with stories of her youth, and when she was laughing hard and out of breath he did the same. It was interesting to learn they had both been rebellious as children and teenagers.

"I guess you had to rein in all that when you took over the company from your grandfather? Can't have a respectable CEO wreaking havoc, right?" she asked and laughed.

Daniel grinned. "I guess not. Although I wasn't quite the wayward teen that you were. No tattoos...so I was nowhere near as hardcore as you."

She laughed again. "That's only because you're scared of needles."

"No need to rub it in. I'm well aware of my weakness."

She rested her elbows on the table and sighed. "You don't have a weak bone in your body."

He met her gaze. "I have a weakness for you."

"That's not weakness," she said. "That's desire. Attraction. Lust."

Daniel pushed his plate aside. "Maybe it's more than that."

"More?"

He reached across the table and grasped her hand. "I care about you."

"Because I'm having your babies," she said, and went to move her hand.

Daniel's grip tightened. "That's only part of it."

She looked at him, her eyes suddenly all suspicious as she pulled her hand free. "What are you saying?"

He met her gaze. "Can't you guess?"

"I don't understand. Are you saying that you're... That you have feelings for me...?"

"Yes," he replied. "That's precisely what I'm saying."

Her gaze widened. "Are you saying that...that you're in love with me?"

Daniel nodded. That was exactly what he was saying. He *did* love her. The empty feeling he had inside when he was away from her was love. That was why he couldn't wait to return to Crystal Point. He wanted her. He craved her and ached thinking about it. She was the mother of his babies. And she was vivacious and fun and as sexy as anything.

He'd loved Simone. It had made sense. Loving Mary-Jayne made no sense at all. And yet, in the past few days it had become a clear and undeniable truth.

"Would it be so hard to believe?"

"Yes. Impossible," she said with a scowl and pushed the chair back. "I think you should leave."

Daniel got to his feet the same time she did. "Why are you angry?"

She glared at him. "Because you're lying to me. Because you'll say and do anything to get what you want and all of a sudden you seem to think that making some big statement about love will make me change my mind about getting married."

"I haven't mentioned marriage," he reminded her.

"It's on the agenda, though, right?"

"Eventually," he replied. "That's generally the result of a relationship between two people who fall in love."

"But *two* people haven't fallen in love."

Right. So she didn't love him. Didn't care. That was plain enough. His heart sank. Maybe she would... someday? If he tried hard enough to earn that love.

"We could try to make this work."

"Like your parents did?" she asked. "Maybe it worked for them because they actually liked one another to start with. I'll bet they didn't call one another names and look for the worst in each other."

Daniel expelled an impatient breath. "I apologized for what I said the last time I was here."

"You mean when you called me a fraud who had locked herself in a cage?" she enquired, brows up, temper on alert. "Don't be... You were right. I have been in a cage, Daniel. But as of this moment I'm out of it. And do you know what...I'm not going to trade one cage for another. Because being married to you would put me right back inside."

"I don't want to keep you caged, Mary-Jayne. I love your spirit and your—"

"Can you hear yourself? Three weeks ago you were calling me a flake and a gold digger and now you've miraculously fallen in love with me. I'm not stupid. I know when I'm being played. So you can come here with your sexy smile and make dinner and act all interested in my childhood and this town, but it doesn't change one undeniable fact—you want me to marry you because it suits you and your arrogant assumption that you can simply take whatever you want. Well, you can't take me."

He took a step toward her, but she moved backward. "What do I have to say to convince you that I'm serious about my feelings for you?"

"Say?" she echoed. "Nothing. Words are empty. It's actions that matter."

He waved an arm. "I'm here, aren't I? I came back. I feel as if I've been pursuing you for months."

"You first chased me because you wanted to get me into bed," she said hotly. "And now you're chasing me because you want your sons."

"I'm chasing you because I love you."

There... It was out on the table...for her and her alone.

She laughed, but it sounded hollow. "You're chasing me because you think it's a means to an end. Well, forget it. What I want for my life I can't get from you."

Pain ripped through his chest. "How do you know that? Just tell me what you want."

"I've told you in half a dozen ways. I want a man who carries me here," she said and put her hand against her breast. "In his heart. Over his heart. On his heart. Forever. And it might sound sentimental and foolish to you, but I don't care. I think I really know that for the first time in my life. And I have you to thank for it. You've shown me what I want...and what I don't."

"And what you don't want...that's me?" he asked, aching through to his bones.

"Yes," she said quietly. "Exactly."

He moved closer and grasped her shoulders, gripping her firmly. And then he kissed her. Long and hot and loaded with pain and guilt and resentment. When he was done he lifted his head and stared down into her face. She was breathing hard and her eyes were filled with confusion and rage.

He ran a possessive hand down her shoulder and breast and then down to her belly. "Nothing will change the fact that a part of me is growing inside you. Love me or hate me, we're bound together. And we always will be."

Chapter Twelve

The following Saturday, it was her niece's second birthday and Mary-Jayne didn't have the strength of mind to go, or to excuse herself. She'd exiled herself in her little house for five days, working on new pieces, revamping her website, thinking of her work, her babies and little else. She didn't spare a thought for Daniel. Not one. Not a single, solitary thought.

Big, fat liar...

He was in her dreams. She couldn't keep him out.

He'd said he loved her. It should have made her day. It should have...but didn't. It only made her angry. And achingly sad.

He hadn't contacted her. She knew from Evie that he wasn't staying at the B and B, and could only assume that he was at a hotel somewhere in Bellandale. It suited her just fine. She didn't want to see him. Not yet. She was still reeling from his declaration of love. Still hating him for it. And still loving him more than she had imagined she could ever love anyone.

Jerk...

Plus, her belly was getting bigger every day and now she waddled rather than walked. She went shopping for baby clothes with her sisters and cried all the way home because she felt as though part of her was missing. She considered buying furniture for the nursery and then put the idea on hold. The spare room needed significant work. In fact, she wondered how she was supposed to raise two babies in such a small house. Once she put two cribs, a change table and a cupboard in the spare room there wouldn't be much space for anything else. What she needed was a bigger house. With a large yard. With a swing set that the twins would be able to play on when they were old enough.

She felt a sense of loneliness so acute it physically pained her. And nothing abated it. Not her parents or her sisters. Not talking to her long-distance friends or cuddling with her dog on the lounge. Only her babies growing peacefully in her belly gave her comfort.

On the afternoon of the party she laid her dress on the bed, flicked off her flip-flops and started getting ready. The dress was a maternity smock in bright colored silk that tied in a knot at her nape, and the outrageously red sandals were low heeled and comfortable. Or at least they would have been, had she been able to get them on. Her body simply wouldn't bend like it used to. She twisted and turned herself inside out and still the darn sandals wouldn't clasp.

Frustration crept over her skin as she kept trying. And failing. Fifteen minutes later and she was ready to toss the shoes at the wall. Until the tears came. Great racking sobs that made her chest hurt. After a few minutes she couldn't actually remember why she was crying. Which only made her more emotional. More fraught. More miserable.

She considered calling Evie and then quickly changed her mind. Her sister had enough to do organizing the party. And Grace had a newborn and would be too busy. She thought about calling her brother, but once he saw she'd been crying he'd be all concerned and want to know why she was upset and then act all macho when she told him how much she hated and loved Daniel. He'd probably want to go and punch him in the nose. It would serve Daniel right, too. Although she was pretty sure he'd throw a punch as good as he got.

Not that she wanted to see him hurt. That was the last thing she wanted.

She sat on the edge of the bed and cried some more. And thought about how ridiculously she was behaving. And then cried again. She gave the shoes another try and gave up when her aching back and swollen feet wouldn't do what she wanted.

She flopped back on the bed and grabbed her phone. The battery signal beeped. She'd forgotten to charge it overnight. Typical. She flicked through the numbers and reached the one she wanted. After a few unanswered rings it went straight to message service.

"It's me," she said, and hiccupped. "Can you come over?"

Then she buried her head in the pillow and sobbed.

Daniel had been in the shower when Mary-Jayne called. He tried to call her back several times but it went to message. Unable to reach her back, he was dressed and out the door of his hotel in about two minutes flat. He drove to Crystal Point as speedily as he could without breaking the law. Pulling up outside her house, he jumped out and raced to the front door. No one answered when he knocked. He heard the little dog barking behind the door and panic set in behind his ribs. What if she was hurt? Perhaps she'd fallen over trying to lift something heavy? Or worse. He rattled the door but it was locked, and then saw that the front window was open. He pushed the screen in and climbed through, not caring if the neighbors thought he was an intruder. They could call the cops for all he cared. He just needed to know she was safe.

Once he was in the living room he called her name. Still nothing.

He got to her bedroom door and stilled in his tracks. She was on the bed, curled up.

He'd never moved so fast in his life. He was beside the bed in seconds. He said her name softly and touched her bare shoulder. Her red-rimmed eyes flicked open.

"Hey," he said and stroked her cheek. "What's wrong?"

She shook her head. "Nothing."

"You left a message on my cell."

"I know," she whispered. "I didn't know who else to call. And then you didn't call back and then my phone went dead and…" Her voice trailed off.

Daniel's stomach churned. He grasped her shoulders. "Mary-Jayne, what's wrong? Are you sick? Is it the babies?"

"I'm not sick," she said. "I'm fine. The babies are fine."

She didn't look fine. She looked as if she'd been crying for a week. But she'd called him. She'd reached out when he'd feared she never would. It was enough to give him hope. To make him believe that she did care. "You've been crying?"

She nodded as tears welled in her eyes. She hiccupped. "I couldn't…"

"You couldn't what?" he prompted.

"I couldn't get my shoes on!"

And then she sobbed. Racking, shuddering sobs that reached him deep down. He folded her in his arms and held her gently. "It's okay, darling," he assured her.

"I'm as fat as a house."

"You're beautiful."

"I'm not," she cried, tears running down her face again. "And my ankles are so swollen that my shoes don't fit. I tried to put them on but my belly got in the way."

Daniel relaxed his grip and reached for her chin. He tilted her head back. "Would you like me to put them on for you?"

She nodded, and he moved off the bed and found her shoes by the wall. He crouched by the bed and reached for her legs. He slipped the shoes on and strapped each sandal at the ankle. "See...they fit just fine," he said, and ran a palm down her smooth calf.

She hiccupped and some fire returned to her eyes. "Why are you being nice to me?"

"That's my job," he said, and sat beside her. "Isn't that why you called me?"

She shrugged helplessly. "I just called a number... Any number..."

He grasped her chin again and made her look at him. "You called *me* because you wanted me here."

She sighed. "I don't know why. Probably because I was dreaming about you and—"

"Good," he said, feeling possessive and frustrated. "I want you to dream about me. I ache to be in your dreams, Mary-Jayne," he rasped, and pulled her close. "I won't be kept out of them."

"I couldn't keep you out if I tried," she admitted, and then relaxed against him, despite her better judgment, he suspected. "I don't know what's wrong with me. I feel so—"

"You're pregnant," he said, and gently spread a hand over her stomach. "Your hormones are running riot. Don't beat yourself up about being emotional. It's perfectly normal."

Her eyes flashed. "Aren't you Mr. Sensitive all of a sudden?"

Daniel's mouth curled at the edges. "With you, absolutely."

"Only to get what you want," she said and sniffed. "Now who's the fraud?"

He tilted her chin again and inched his mouth closer to hers. "I really did screw up, didn't I, for you to have such a low opinion of me? I generally think of myself as a good sort of person, Mary-Jayne... Give me half a chance and you might, too."

She harrumphed. "Manipulative jerk," she whispered, but then moved her lips closer.

He kissed her gently. "I'm not manipulating you. I love you."

She moaned. "Don't say things you don't mean."

Daniel swept her hair back from her face. "I mean it. And I'll tell you every day for the rest of my life."

"I won't listen," she retorted, and tried to evade his mouth. "And one day I'll find someone who really does—"

"Don't do that," he said painfully, cutting through her words. "That would just about break me."

"I'll do what I want," she said and pulled back. "You don't own me."

Daniel held her still. "Oh, darling...I do. And you own me. You've owned me since the first time I saw you in that store window. And I'm not going anywhere, Mary-Jayne."

"You'll have to at some point," she remarked, all eyes

and fiery beauty in her stare. "You don't live here. You live in San Francisco. Then I'll be free of you."

"We'll never be free of one another. That's why you called me today. Admit it," he said, firmer this time. "You could have called any one of half a dozen people and they all would have been here in a matter of minutes. But you didn't," he reminded her. "You called me."

"It was the first number I pressed. It was random, and then my battery died. Don't read anything into it."

He chuckled, delighted and spurred on by her reticence. "Admit it… You're in love with me."

"I am not!" she denied, and pulled herself from his arms. "I don't love you. I never will. I'd have to be stark raving mad to fall in love with you. And you're only saying all this to get what you want."

"I am? Really?" He stood up and propped his hands on his hips. "Have I asked for anything? I've given you space. I've left you alone. I've holed myself up in a damn hotel room for a week, even though all I want to do is be here with you every day and hold you in my arms every night. I haven't sent you flowers or bought anything for the babies even though I want to because I know you'd accuse me of trying to manipulate you. I haven't gone to see your parents and explain to them what you mean to me and assure them I'll do whatever is in my power to do to make you happy even though my instincts tell me I should. I'm *trying*, Mary-Jayne… I'm trying to do this your way. Just… just try to meet me in the middle somewhere, okay?" He placed a hand over his chest. "Because this is killing me."

"So he's still in town?"

Mary-Jayne looked at Evie. Her sisters had come over to cheer her up and bring her some gifts for the babies. The tiny pair of matching baseball caps Grace gave her was so incredibly cute that she cried a little. Which seemed to have become a habit of hers in the past few weeks.

Crying... Ugh!

She had become a sentimental sap.

"I guess so."

"You've seen him?" Grace asked.

"Not for a week. Why?"

Her sisters both shrugged and smiled. It was Evie who spoke next. "It's only that...well... In the past few days he's come to see all of us and told us..."

"Told you all what?" Mary-Jayne asked, pushing up on her seat.

"That he's in love with you," Grace supplied. "That he wants to marry you."

Mary-Jayne saw red. "That no-good, sneaky—"

"It's kinda romantic," Evie said and grinned.

"It's *not* romantic," Mary-Jayne said hotly. "It's deceitful and underhanded. And do you know what else he did? He bought all this baby stuff and had it delivered. The garage is full of boxes and toys and baby furniture and—"

"Oh, how awful for you," Evie said and grinned. "Such a terrible man."

Mary-Jayne scowled. "You're on his side, then?"

"We're on your side," Grace said and smiled gently. "You seem unhappy, that's all."

"I'll be happier when he's gone."

"I don't think he's going anywhere any time soon," Evie said. "He told Scott he's going to buy a house here."

The color bled from her face. "I don't believe it. He wouldn't. He's got a business to run and he can't do that from here."

"Maybe he's found something more important than business," Grace said pointedly.

"Yeah—his heirs. He wants his children. Don't be blinded by the good looks and money."

"We could say the same thing to you."

Mary-Jayne stilled. Her sister's words resonated loud and clear. Was that how she appeared—as a judgmental and narrow-minded snob—and exactly what she'd accused him of being?

She'd resented his money and success without good reason. On one hand, she recognized his honesty and integrity. And yet, when he'd told her the very thing she wanted to hear, she hadn't believed him. She'd accused him of trying to manipulate and confuse her. But what proof did she have that he'd ever done that? None. He hadn't manipulated her to get her into bed. Their attraction had been hot and intense from the start. Not one-sided. She'd craved him and he'd made it abundantly clear that he wanted her. And then she'd convinced herself he was all bad, all arrogance and self-entitlement.

To protect herself.

Because he was nothing like any man she'd previously dated she regarded him as an aberration…someone to avoid…someone to battle. And she had at every opportunity. She'd fought and insulted and pushed him away time and time again. Because loving Daniel meant she would be redefined. He was rich and successful and all that she had professed to loathe. He'd asked her to marry him. He'd said he loved her. And still she let her prejudice blind her.

His parting words a week earlier still echoed in her mind. *This is killing me.* Real pain. Real anguish. And she'd done that to him. She'd hurt him. She'd hurt the one person she loved most in the world. She felt the shame of it through to her bones. He'd asked her to meet him in the middle.

But she could do better than that.

"You look as though the proverbial penny just dropped," Evie said.

Both her sisters were staring at her. "I think it just did. He asked me to marry him. He said he was in love with me."

"That's what he told us, too."

Tears filled her eyes. "I never imagined that I'd fall in love with someone like him. I thought that one day I'd meet someone like myself... Someone who wasn't so... conventional, if you know what I mean."

Evie came and sat beside her and grabbed her hand. "You know, just because he's not a bohemian poet, it doesn't make him wrong for you. If anyone had told me a few years ago that I would fall in love with a man nearly ten years younger than me I wouldn't have believed them."

"Same here," Grace said, and sat on the other side. "I never intended to fall in love with our brother's best friend. But I did. When you love, you simply love. That's the thing that's important, M.J. Not how successful or wealthy he is."

"He's a good man," Evie said quietly. "Give him a chance to prove it."

"What if he's changed his mind?" she asked, thinking of the terrible way they'd parted and how she'd told him she didn't love him and never would. "I said some pretty awful things to him the last time we were together. What if he doesn't want to see me?"

"You need a plan," Grace suggested.

"Leave that to me," Evie said, and she grabbed her phone from her bag.

Three hours later Mary-Jayne was at the B and B, sitting in the garden on a bench by the wishing well. She smoothed down the skirt on her white dress and then fluffed her hair. She'd always loved this spot. Through the vine-covered hedge she saw a car pull up to the curb.

Minutes later he was walking up the path, all purposeful and tight limbed. He wore jeans and a polo shirt and looked so good it stole her breath. When he spotted her he came to a halt midstride.

"Hi," she said, and smiled.

His expression was unreadable. "I didn't expect you to be here."

"I didn't expect me to be here up until a couple of hours ago."

His gaze narrowed. "Are you all right? No problems with the babies?"

She touched her abdomen gently. "No… Everything is fine. I feel good. The nausea is gone for the moment. I haven't seen you for a while… Where have you been?"

"I was under the impression you had no interest in seeing me." He took a step closer. "I had a call from your sister. Is she here?"

"No…just me."

His brows drew together. "Subterfuge?"

"Kind of," she admitted. "I wasn't sure if *you'd* see *me* after the last time."

"If you had called me, I would be here. Always. I've told you that before. What's this about, Mary-Jayne?"

He looked so good. So familiar. And she ached to be in his arms. "I'm sorry about what I said the last time we were together."

"Which part? When you said you didn't love me and never would?" he quizzed.

She nodded. "All of it. You came over to help me and I was thoughtless and ungrateful."

"Yes, you were."

She ignored a hot niggle of impatience that crept up her spine. "I hear you're looking at real estate?"

He shrugged loosely. "Do you disapprove of that, as well?"

God, he was impossible. "Of course not. I understand that you'll want to be close to the babies when they are born."

He nodded. "So anything else?"

Mary-Jayne sighed and grabbed the shopping bag by the bench. She stood up and extracted the two tiny baseballs caps. "I thought you might like these. They're cute, don't you think?"

He took the caps and examined them. "Cute. Yes. Is that it? You got me here to give me a couple of baseball caps?"

"I wanted to see you."

"Why now? Nothing's changed."

"Everything's changed."

His mouth flattened. "What?"

Her cheeks grew hotter by the second. "Me. This. Us. A week ago you told me you loved me."

"I know what I said," he shot back. "I also know what you said."

She took a breath. "Shall we go inside? I'd like to talk to you."

"So when you want to talk, we talk? Is that how this plays out? I don't seem to be able to get it right with you, do I?"

Mary-Jayne let her impatience rise up. "I'm going inside. You can stay out here in the garden and sulk if you want to."

She turned on her heels and walked up to the house as quickly as she could. He was about four steps behind her. Once she was through the French doors and in the living room she spun around.

He was barely a foot away, chest heaving. "Sulk?"

She shrugged. "Sure. Isn't that what you've been doing

this week? So I said something mean and unkind. I'm sorry. But you said yourself that I'm running on hormones because of my pregnancy. I should think it's about time you started making allowances for that."

"Allowances," he echoed incredulously. "Are you serious? I've done nothing *but* make allowances since the moment you told me you were pregnant. Nothing I do is right. Nothing I say makes any difference. You trust me, you don't. You need me, you don't. You want me, you don't. Which is it? I'm so damned confused I can barely think straight. I'm neglecting my business, my family, my friends…everything, because I'm so caught up in this *thing* I have with you."

Mary-Jayne watched him, fascinated by the heat and fire in his words. There was so much passion in him. She'd been so wrong, thinking he was some sort of cold fish who didn't feel deeply. He did. He just didn't show that side of himself to the world.

"I do trust you," she said, and moved toward him. "And I do need you," she said, and touched his chest. When he winced and stepped back she was immediately concerned. "What's wrong? Are you in pain? Have you had another migraine?"

"No. Stop this, Mary-Jayne. Tell me what I'm doing here and—"

"I'm trying," she said frantically. "But I need to know if you meant what you said."

He frowned. "What I said?"

"You…you said you loved me," she said, suddenly breathless. "Did you mean it?"

"Do I strike you as someone who says things I don't mean?"

"No," she replied, and blinked back the tears in her eyes. "It's just that…what you said about me being in a cage and about how things would have been different from the start if you hadn't been...well...*you*. If you'd been a dreadlocked, unemployed musician, I wouldn't have been so determined to keep my distance. Because that's what I thought I wanted. What I knew, if that makes sense. All that stuff you said, you were right." She touched his arm, gripped tightly and felt his muscles hard beneath her palm. "For as long as I can remember I've craved freedom and independence. But now I feel as if I've lived a life that isn't authentic. I left home at seventeen, but only moved three streets away from my parents. Some independence, huh? So you're right, I'm a fraud. I'm tied to this little town. I'm not a free spirit at all." She took a breath, not caring about the tears on her cheeks. "And you...you saw through that and through me. What you said about marriage makes sense. Each one starts out differently, like your dad and Bernie. And if this..." she said, and touched her stomach gently. "If this is what we start with, just these two precious babies bringing us together, then that's okay. Because if you do want me, and if you do love me, even a little bit, that will be enough."

He stared at her, holding her gaze captive. "But it's not enough for me, Mary-Jayne."

She froze. "I don't understand..."

"We both deserve more than some half-baked attempt at a relationship."

"But you said you wanted to get married and be a family," she reminded him, crumbling inside.

"I do," he said, and grabbed her hand. "But I want *all* of you, every beautiful, spirited, intoxicating piece. I had a good marriage once. But I want more than that this time. I don't want to leave at six in the morning and arrive home at eight. I don't want to eat out five nights out of seven because work always comes first. I don't want to miss family gatherings because I'm too busy landing some deal or flying from one country to the next. I've lived that life and I was never truly happy. I want us to raise our children together, like *they* deserve."

Tears wet her cheeks again. "I want that, too. You really... You really do love me?"

He grasped her chin and looked directly into her eyes. "I really do love you, Mary-Jayne. And I know they're only words, but they are what I feel."

"Words are enough," she said, happiness surging through her blood. "I love you, too."

"Words will never be enough," he said, and kissed her gently. "Which is why I did this."

"What?" she muttered against his mouth.

"This," he said, and stepped back a little. He tugged at the collar of his T-shirt and showed her what he meant.

Her name, in small but strikingly dark scrolled script, was now written on the left side of his chest. The ink was new and still healing, but she could see through all that to the beauty of what he had done.

"You got a tattoo?" she asked, crying. "I can't believe you did that. The needles... You hate needles."

He shrugged one shoulder. "I love you more than I hate needles." He grasped her hand and held it against his chest. "In my heart. Over my heart. On my heart. Forever."

They were the most beautiful words she had ever heard.

She reached up and touched his face. "I'm so much in love with you, Daniel. And I'm sorry I kept pushing you away."

He held her in his arms. "You had more sense than me. We needed to get to know one another. You knew that. I just arrogantly thought I knew how to fix things."

"At least you wanted to try," she said, and settled against

his shoulder. "I've been fighting this and you since the very beginning."

"I know," he said, and laughter rumbled in his chest. "You took off as if your feet were on fire after Solana's birthday party."

"I was in shock," she admitted. "I'd never had an experience like that before."

"Me, either," he said. "Making love with you is like nothing on earth." He kissed her nape. "But you never have to run from me again, Mary-Jayne."

"I promise I won't."

Seconds later they were settled on one of the sofas and he wrapped her in his arms. "There's something about you that draws me. You have this incredible energy…a life force all your own. I love that about you. And I love that our sons are going to have that, too."

She sighed, happy and content and so in love her head was spinning. "So where are we going to live? Here or San Francisco?"

He reached for her chin and tilted her face toward his own. "Darling, do you think I would ever ask you to leave here? This is your home."

"But San Francisco is *your* home."

"It's where I live," he said and kissed her gently. "I don't think I've ever considered anywhere as really home. Until now. Even when I was married to Simone and we had our apartment, most times it was simply a place to sleep."

She couldn't believe what he was saying. "Do you mean we can stay here permanently? I was imagining we'd do some time here and some over there."

He shook his head. "Your family is here. Your roots are here. And I like this town and I want to raise our sons here. If they turn out half as good as you then I'll be a happy man."

"But your business? How can you—"

"I need to let go a little," he admitted. "I need to trust Blake and Caleb more. They have just as must invested in Anderson's as I do... I think it's about time I lessened the reins. You see," he said, and grinned, "I'm learning to not be so much of a control freak."

"Don't change too much," she said, and pressed against him. "I like you just as you are."

He kissed her, long and sweet, and when he finally lifted his head he stared into her eyes. "You know something...I think it's time I proposed properly."

"What a great idea," she said, and laughed, so happy she thought she might burst.

Daniel grabbed her hand and brought it to his lips. "Mary-Jayne, I'm lost without you... Marry me?"

"Yes," she said, laughing, crying and loving him more than she had believed possible. "Absolutely, positively, yes!"

Epilogue

Three and a half months later...

At seven o'clock at night on a Monday, Mary-Jayne's water broke. Daniel was walking into the bedroom when he hovered in the bathroom doorway.

"What is it?" he asked immediately.

She grimaced. "It's time."

Panic flittered across his face. "You're in labor?"

"Yep," she said, and grinned.

He strode toward her. "But there's still nearly three weeks to go."

"We were told I'd probably go into labor early," she said and touched his arm. "Stop worrying."

"I'm not worried," he assured her. "How do you feel?"

"Better now I know what the niggling backache I had all day is about."

"You were in pain and you didn't tell—"

"Stop worrying," she said again, and ushered him o
the doorway. "I'm fine." She rubbed her huge belly. "We'
fine. Is my bag still in the car?"

He'd insisted they have her baby bag ready for whe
she went into labor. He'd also insisted on a trial run in th
car and had organized Evie to be the backup driver ju
in case he wasn't around when the time came. Of cours
she knew that was never going to happen.

In the past few months so much had changed. Sinc
their wedding two months earlier, he'd taken some muc
needed time off from Anderson's. His brother Blake ha
taken on more global accountability, and general mar
agers had been put in place in some of the resorts to a
leviate the workload. Caleb was still recovering from
unexpected and serious boating accident and had bee
recuperating from his busted leg with Miles and Bern
for the past eight weeks. It had been a fraught time for th
entire family, but since Bernie's heart attack, the fami
had become closer and they all rallied around to ensu
Caleb had all the support he needed.

Despite all that, she knew Daniel had never been ha
pier. She still marveled at how well he'd adjusted to n
having such tight control over the company anymore. He
learned to trust his brothers and share the responsibilit
Of course, with Caleb out of action for a while, there we
times when he was needed to fly back to San Francisco
one of the other locations, but he was never gone for mo
than a few days. And Mary-Jayne didn't mind.

He'd bought a house in Crystal Point just four doo
down from Dunn Inn, and she loved the big low-set bric
and-tile home with its floating timber floors, racked cei
ings, wide doorways and sprawling front deck that offer
an incredible view of the ocean. She surprised herself
how much fun she had purchasing new furnishings.

was generous to a fault, and they had a wonderful time working on the nursery and getting the room ready for the babies.

Their relationship was amazing. *He* was amazing, and she'd never been happier.

The drive to the hospital took twenty minutes, and another five to find a vacant car space and get her into the emergency ward. She was quickly transported to maternity, and by the time she was settled in a room her contractions were coming thick and fast.

It was an arduous twelve hours later that her doctor recommended a caesarean birth. Mary-Jayne cried a little, and then agreed to do what best for their babes. William and Flynn Anderson were born a minute apart, both pink and screaming and perfect in every way.

Still groggy from the surgery, it was another few hours before she had a chance to nurse her sons. Daniel remained by her side, strong and resilient and giving her every ounce of support she needed. And when he held their sons for the first time, there were tears in his eyes. And he didn't seem to care one bit. Watching him, seeing the emotion and pure love in his expression made her fall in love with him even more.

"They really are beautiful," she remarked as William settled against her breast to nurse and Daniel sat in the chair by her bed and held Flynn against his chest.

Daniel looked at his son, marveling at the perfect beauty in the little boy's face, and smiled. When he returned his gaze to his wife he saw she was watching him. "You did an amazing job, Mrs. Anderson."

She smiled. "You, too. But then again, you do everything well, and I knew this wouldn't be any different."

Daniel reached for her hand and rubbed her fingers. You know, we're going to have to start letting the masses in at some point. Your sisters are keen to spend some time with you. And Solana has been circling the waiting area with your parents for the past two hours. She's very excited about meeting her great-grandsons."

"I know," she said, and sighed. "I just selfishly want our babies and you to myself for as long as I can."

Daniel stood and gently placed their sleeping son into his mother's arm, watching, fascinated, as she held them both. It was the most beautiful thing he had ever seen. His wife. His sons. They were a gift more precious than anything he could have ever imagined. Love, the purest and most intense he'd ever experienced, surged through his blood.

"I love you," he said, and bent down to kiss her sweet mouth. "And, my darling, you have me to yourself for the rest of our lives."

Tears welled in her beautiful green eyes. "I never intended to love anyone this much, you know," she said, and batted her lashes. "I never thought it was possible."

"Neither did I."

"It's actually all Audrey and Caleb's doing," she said, beaming. "If they didn't have such a dysfunctional relationship we would never have met."

"Oh, I don't know about that," he said, and chuckled "Audrey would have returned to Crystal Point eventually and Caleb would have eventually followed her, and since my brother is a hothead without any sense I would have had to come here and sort things out. So I'm pretty sure our paths would have crossed."

Mary-Jayne glanced at the twins. "Maybe you're right Now they're here I can't imagine a world without these two in it." She looked up and smiled gently. "Speaking of Caleb and Audrey...any news?"

Daniel shrugged. "You know Caleb. He's refusing to get the marriage annulled."

They had all been shocked to learn that Caleb and Audrey were in fact married, and had been just a month after they'd met.

She sighed. "Well, I'm glad we don't have all that drama in our relationship."

Daniel smiled, remembering their own fraught beginnings. "Nah...we were a piece of cake."

She laughed, and the lovely sound echoed around the room.

"Shall I let them in?" he asked, kissing her again.

"You bet."

And he was, he realized as he opened the door, just about the happiest man on the planet. Because he had Mary-Jayne's love and their beautiful sons. He truly did have it all.

* * * * *

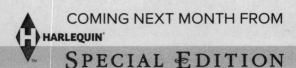

COMING NEXT MONTH FROM

HARLEQUIN®

SPECIAL EDITION

Available April 21, 2015

#2401 NOT QUITE MARRIED

The Bravos of Justice Creek • by Christine Rimmer

After a fling with Dalton Ames on an idyllic island, Clara Bravo wound up pregnant. She never told Dalton the truth, since the recently divorced hunk insisted he wasn't interested in a relationship. But when Dalton discovers Clara's secret, he's determined to create a forever-after with the Bravo beauty and their baby...no matter how much she protests!

#2402 MY FAIR FORTUNE

The Fortunes of Texas: Cowboy Country
by Nancy Robards Thompson

On the outside, PR guru Brodie Fortune Hayes is the perfect British gentleman. But on the inside, he's not as polished as he seems. When Brodie is hired to fix up the image of Horseback Hollow's Cowboy Country theme park, one lovely Texan—his former fling Caitlyn Moore—might just be the woman who can open his heart after all!

#2403 A FOREVER KIND OF FAMILY

Those Engaging Garretts! • by Brenda Harlen

Daddy. That's one role Ryan Garrett never thought he'd occupy...until his friend's death left him with custody of a fourteen-month-old. He definitely didn't count on gorgeous Harper Ross stepping in to help with little Oliver. As they butt heads and sparks fly, another Garrett bachelor finds the love of a lifetime!

#2404 FOLLOWING DOCTOR'S ORDERS

Texas Rescue • by Caro Carson

Dr. Brooke Brown has devoted her entire life to her career—but that doesn't mean she isn't susceptible to playboy firefighter Zach Bishop's smoldering good looks. A fling soon turns into so much more, but Brooke's tragic past and Zach's newly discovered future might stand in the way of the family they've always wanted.

#2405 FROM BEST FRIEND TO BRIDE

The St. Johns of Stonerock • by Jules Bennett

Police chief Cameron St. John has always loved his best friend, Megan Richards—and not just in a platonic way. But there's too much baggage for friendship to turn into romance, so Cameron sets his feelings aside...until Megan's life is threatened by her dangerous brother. Then Cameron will stop at nothing to protect her—and ensure their future together.

#2406 HIS PREGNANT TEXAS SWEETHEART

Peach Leaf, Texas • by Amy Woods

Katie Bloom has fallen on hard times. She's pregnant and alone, and the museum where she works is going out of business. Now Ryan Ford, the one who got away, walks into a local eatery, tempting her with his soulful good looks. Ryan's got secret but can he put Katie and her child above everything else to create a lifelong love?

HSECNM0415